THE HALF LIFE

Mark Wesley

THE HALF LIFE OF HARRY FIGG

Novel Published by Mark Wesley
Text © Mark Wesley 2024

Screenplay published by Mark Wesley
Dec 2020
WGA West Reg: 2091840

All rights reserved. No part of this publication may be reproduced, stored in a retrieval system, or transmitted in any form or by any means, electronic, electrostatic, recording, magnetic tape, mechanical, photocopying or otherwise, without prior permission in writing from the publisher. All characters in this book are fictitious and any resemblance to real persons, living or dead, is entirely coincidental.

Mark Wesley has asserted his right under the Copyright, Designs and Patents Act, 1988 to be identified as the author of this work

Copyright © 2024 Mark Wesley
All rights reserved.

ISBN- 9798878423717

THE HALF LIFE OF HARRY FIGG

More thrilling Mark Wesley novels are available from Amazon in both paperback and Kindle formats. BANGK! is also available as an audio book.

Visit markwesley.net

The Half Life of Harry Figg

The Half Life of Harry Figg

Prologue

Night time in Jorden County in the magnolia and honeysuckle scented embrace of late summer is a hot and humid affair, prone to thunderstorms rumbling in from the Gulf and the irritating attention of no-see-ums. You get used to all three, given time.

None of that seemed to bother the old bulldog as he sprayed another tree to mark its territory. He'd given the same loving attention to most of the ancient oaks along the avenue during his regular evening walks over the years.

It amused his owner to imagine a fat Cuban cigar, like the one he was smoking, planted in the old dog's jaws. He reckoned he'd look just like that famous old cigar-smoking Brit, the World War Two leader, Churchill. But it'd be a sad waste of a cigar.

He drew on the stogie and slowly let the aromatic smoke escape in a satisfying exhale. It rose up all lazy and wraith like until it was snatched away by a sudden warm gust.

He tugged the leash.

"Come on, Winston. Attaboy."

The mutt grudgingly brought his business to an end and did his masters bidding. His four short legs cantering to keep up.

His master, an elderly man, still fit enough to enjoy a regular stroll in one of the old towns few swanky addresses looked up as a spot of rain fell.

"Well, old boy, looks like we're in for another soaking. Maybe we should head home. What do you say, old fella?"

Nothing from the dog. Just more tongue lolling, gasping and a wag of his stubby tail.

Despite the threat of rain, they walked on a little further.

As pleasant as the old street was with its historic single-family homes set in manicured yards, the one eye-sore that every resident complained about was the one they were passing just then. The owners had allowed it to sink into near dereliction. The one rotten tooth in a Hollywood smile.

Not a lick of paint or wood preserver had been spent on the property in decades. The yard was overgrown. Some subscribe to the idea of letting nature have its way, but this was just an untidy mess.

They stopped for a moment as Winston snuffled along the grass verge searching for that indefinable place for a pee. A spot that an inch either side would be unsuitable. He raised his leg and missed anyway.

That's when the entire neighborhood power went out.

With the sky clouded over and the street lights out, it was as black as pitch. The only light seemed to come from behind the nineteen-twenties clapboard ruin they were standing in front of.

It was a strange sight. Something the old man hadn't witnessed before. The house was a shadowy silhouette against a shimmering violet glow. Without that halo of light, the house would have been as invisible in the darkness as all the others in the avenue.

Another spot of rain ran down his cheek. He wiped it off.

"You know boy, that's real peculiar. It don't seem natural."

Winston was busy sniffing the grass again.

"How about we take a look see? You want a walk through the long grass?"

It wasn't a negotiation. He pushed the broken gate open and set off to beat a path around the house. The old bulldog didn't complain. This was something new. He kept trying to dart off in different directions attracted by the rustling of wildlife in the neglected shrubbery. The retractable leash held him in check.

As they came to an old wooden shed the light seemed brighter, but now a low humming sound could be heard.

A few more steps and the sight that greeted them as they turned the corner brought both man and dog to an astonished standstill.

Winston gave a low menacing growl.

The back yard was floodlit by a brilliant spear of incandescent violet light streaking out of the window of a room high in the house.

It flickered and pulsed as the low droning hum grew in intensity.

Just as suddenly both the light and the noise snapped off, as though a switch had been thrown.

Total darkness for a moment and then, one by one, street lights and house lights came back on. Everything was back to normal again. Like nothing had happened.

He felt another couple of drops of rain – then a few more. He drew some smoke from the last inch of the cigar.

"Well, what do you make of that old fella? Strangest thing I ever saw."

Winston just raised his leg and marked the spot.

1

They happen pretty regularly in the southern states, and at this time of year. Storm cells sweeping up from the south dumping what seemed like lakes of water across sparsely populated swamp lands. A vast landscape freckled with small towns.

This storm was no different, except for the time of day. At night in this part of the world the stars usually blaze brilliantly, unquenched by light pollution. But this was a special kind of dark, cruel and complete, that dwelt under the swollen bellies of such huge and oppressive thunderstorms.

***

At first it was just a speck of diffused light flickering and dancing way off on the horizon. Soon, the deserted Jorden County road was filled with the sound of four Goodyears tearing wet tracks out of the storm flooded blacktop.

With its headlights cutting dazzling cones through the deluge the SUV roared past, jazz music wailing loud and fast as it sped on into the darkness.

On board, safe from the sweaty humidity, in air-conditioned comfort, the driver, a petite brunette called Torres, and Roberts, the rangy six-footer sitting next to her, eyed each other with obvious resentment.

Roberts had had just about enough of the random, tuneless – he was going to use the word, 'music' - but he couldn't see how anyone could call the mess of confusion they were listening to, 'music'.

He reached for the radio buttons to find another channel. Bad idea.

Torres threatened, "I swear, if you touch that I'll drag you onto the road and leave you in the rain, crying for your mother."

Chastened, Roberts snatched his hand back like it had been scorched in a fire.

"I can't take any more of this crap. Can't they just play the damn tune?"

"My car. My rules."

"That's just childish."

"I didn't invite you along. Put up with it."

Roberts changed the subject.

"What are you, some kind of private contractor? I don't get it. This operation could have been handled internally."

"Yet here I am," Torres said.

"Well, I'm here so you don't screw up."

"You're here to learn."

***

Except for the jazz radio, they drove in silence for a while. The windshield wipers worked furiously to clear the water, occasionally swiping in time to the beat of the music but making little impact on the torrent hitting the glass.

"You sure you didn't screw up the navigation?" Torres chided Roberts. "This is taking too long."

Through the rain smeared windscreen the headlights caught the smudge of a town name sign.

"Wait a minute! What did that sign say?"

Roberts leaned into the satnav.

"Should be coming up now," said Roberts. "Christ, you ever heard of this place? Random, middle of nowhere dump, on the road to someplace more interesting."

"Yeah, and what backwater glory-hole did you crawl out of, Roberts?"

As they passed the industrial outskirts of the town the skeletal hulk of a derelict warehouse loomed ominously and then was lost in the storm.

The rain eased a little but Roberts was still bitching.

"Jesus, makes Detroit look like a shiny citadel of industrial prosperity."

"When you've finished with the tour guide maybe we should drive past the target before we check in?"

Roberts agreed.

"Works for me."

He went to switch the radio channel again.

"STAY!"

Roberts' hand froze in mid-air.

Watching the road ahead, Torres allowed herself a snarky "Good boy."

2

The Snake Crew were a noisy neighborhood nuisance that loitered on a debris strewn corner lot in the old town suburbs. Their club house was the carcass of a Chevy van, doors missing front and back, and covered in crude Snake Crew graffiti.

Abandoned like an unwanted mutt, it sat forlornly on its wheel hubs. The final indignity.

***

The acne-plagued seventeen-year-old who claimed the title of boss of the outfit, was bolshy Pete 'Snake' McKay, with his snake tattoos and cowboy boots. Next in line to the throne was fifteen-year-old, Benedict 'Baggy' Marchant, who Snake had anointed as his loyal lieutenant.

Next came wiry Lloyd Ferris, the 'artful dodger' to Snake's 'Fagin'. He was always keen to impress the boss, and at fourteen, was a year older than the youngest recruit, Brody Boyle.

It wasn't much to boast about, but for young Brody, the Snake Crew were closer than his own dysfunctional family.

The only difference between him and the other boys, and it was something that jarred with Brody, they didn't see him as a full member of the gang. Maybe it was because he was the youngest. What could he do about that? Not much and anyway, he was only a couple of weeks shy of fourteen.

Maybe he just seemed a bit young for his age, not quite grown up. That awkward time between child and adult.

Brody was watching Snake as he checked the reddened skin around Baggy's new 'serpent' tattoo he had hand-scratched himself just that morning.

"'Bout time you got one Lloyd," Snake said. "You ain't one of the crew, 'less you got a tag. I'll scratch one for you."

He turned to Brody.

"You'n' all Brody."

Mixed emotions for Brody. He wanted the full Snake Crew credentials of a tattoo but the thought of the painful scratching... well, it didn't sound appealing. Brody's hand instinctively went to protect his arm.

***

With the rain easing they clambered out of the van. "Yeah, I'm going to, Snake," said Lloyd as they wandered across the lot to the roadside. "It's just they'll kick me out of school. And Mom..."

Snake jeered.

"Don't be a pussy. What they ever done for you? You don't need 'em. You've got us - Baggy and me."

"And me, Snake," Brody said. "I'm crew ain't I?

"Yeah, well, you aren't yet, you're just... what's that word Bags?"

"Er - what word's that?"

Lloyd piped up.

"Provisional?"

"Yeah, that's it, a provisional member. That's what you are, Brody boy. I gotta come up with something, kid. Some kind of challenge." Snake declared.

Before they could jump out of the way, the SUV sped past, hitting a deep pool of standing water as it motored on down the road. The impact threw a huge sheet of water over the boys, soaking Snake and his precious boots.

"Douche bag!" He yelled as he dried the leather against his jeans. "I tell you Baggy, some people just got bought up bad."

"Got no class," Baggy said.

Lloyd was squeezing the filthy water out of his hoody. "Look at me! The bozo's damn near drowned me."

Baggy laughed. "Quick, give him some soap."

Snake turned to Baggy.

"All this water's given me a thirst," he said meaningfully. "You thirsty Baggs?"

"Now that you mention it..." He looked across to the van. "The mini bar's taken a hit recently."

"Yeah, and room service is a bit unreliable these days," Lloyd said, still wringing water from his clothes.

"Well then, I reckon we'll have to go shopping. You up for a bit of shopping, Brody?"

"I guess so."

"Good, 'cos I've got a job for you."

3

"What's the corporation want with this Figg guy anyway? Roberts said. "I can't see anything here that makes him a person of interest."

Roberts was flicking through the pages of a document as the SUV crept down an avenue of old properties.

Torres said, "Do your homework. It's not the man they're interested in."

Roberts looked enviously at the homes they were passing.

"Wow! This is a ritzy neighborhood. Lots of old money. You can bet the sons and daughters aren't flipping burgers or waiting tables. It'll be Club Med vacations and country club tennis coaches. Maybe some new money too. This is where those mortgage foreclosure profits and Madoff Ponzi schemes ended up."

"Give it a rest, Roberts."

Something snagged her attention just then.

"Wait a minute - that house there."

Torres compared the house to the address on her phone as they drove slowly past.

Set back from the road and hidden by the shade of rotting oaks, long overgrown with Spanish Moss and wild Button Bush, lurked a neglected, double-fronted Tudor Revival house from the nineteen-twenties.

Roberts thought it looked familiar.

"Holy crap! It's the Bates Motel."

Torres agreed, "Let's hope Norm and his crazy old mom aren't in."

4

Not much had changed over the years in the Figg household. It wasn't a home so much as a living museum of furniture and fittings that were old when the sixties were an exciting, new and shiny thing.

In the kitchen, a feeble yellow light from a cracked plastic ceiling lamp cast shadows over curling lino and fifties wallpaper.

Just like the house, the years had taken their toll on Harry Figg. White haired, aged like dried fruit but only fifty-five, Harry was preparing an evening beverage.

A frail voice came from a room upstairs.

"Harry? Harry are you back from school? Tell your sister I want to see her."

"Yes Mom. I'm just making your chocolate," Harry called back patiently.

***

In the darkness, with familiar precision, he stepped over the more dangerous patches of worn stair carpet as he carried a tray of hot chocolate and cookies up to his mother's bedroom.

He turned the worn brass handle, shoved the door open with his hip and entered. Warm tungsten light from a table lamp spilled across the bed sheets. They hid the slight frame of a white-haired woman who was propped up on a pillow. Snuggled alongside her was a pure white Persian cat.

"Where's Harry?"

The anxious enquiry that always came when he entered the room.

He set the tray on the dresser and leaned over to fix his mom's pillow. The fussing irritated the cat. He jumped off of the bed and padded out of the room all high and mighty.

"I'm Harry, Mom," he said gently. "I've got your hot chocolate, just how you like it - nice and sweet."

"I don't like chocolate. I want to talk to your sister."

"You do like chocolate. You always have chocolate."

His mother was becoming agitated.

"Your sister always brings me tea when we come back from the mall."

"Well, she hasn't been here for a long-time mom, has she. Not since..."

His voice faded as it always did when that subject came up.

He took a breath and changed the subject. "How about your talking book? Where were we up to now?"

He switched the player on and a pleasant female voice could be heard reading from somewhere in the middle of a story. Harry turned the volume down a little.

"Where's Schrodinger?" For some reason, the name of the cat was one of the few things she could always recall.

"He's around somewhere." He called out, "Schrodinger! Come on boy."

Nothing from the cat.

As he left the room, he took a final look.

"I'll check back later, OK?"

He closed the door and crossed the landing to his workshop.

***

The room was lit by an anglepoise lamp and the red telltale lights, screens and dials of equipment on a workbench.

His tools were lined up in a precise manner. The way someone troubled by an obsessive compulsive disorder might do.

Harry eased into a battered office chair and turned a page of a notebook. His fingers found a place on the page where he added a quick note in pencil.

He reached over to a collection of buttons, knobs and valves, and threw several switches. His hand grasped a large control and slowly rotated it. Suddenly, the room was ablaze with a violet glow, pulsing and crackling from a glass chamber buried amid a weird collection components. A deep throbbing droning sound filled the lab.

Under the bench, Schrodinger leaped like he'd touched a live wire and scampered out of the room.

5

Behind the counter of a two-aisle minimart a few blocks away, the Asian owner was keeping an eye on a teenager. The boy was meandering up one aisle and down the other and it looked pretty damn suspicious.

With deliberate clumsiness and making sure the store owner saw him, Brody appeared to snatch a handful of candy bars.

The owner moved swiftly from the counter towards the thief.

"Hey! I saw that."

With perfect timing, Brody deliberately hesitated before rushing out into the street. The furious owner raced out after him just as Brody intended. He'd put a little distance between him and the store so the teenager slowed a little to allow the owner to catch up.

The man shouted in frustration. "You kids are always trying to rob me."

Still keeping his distance, Brody showed his empty hands as he turned to taunt him.

"I've done nothing. Leave me alone."

"And what's in your pockets? Show me."

Walking backwards to draw the owner further from his shop, Brody pulled his pockets inside out to show they too were empty.

As he turned and ran, he shouted. "I told you. I haven't stolen nothing."

The owner watched the kid run off into the night, gave a sad sigh of frustration and returned to his store.

But things got worse when he arrived back at the counter. The rear door had been levered open. The same with the tobacco cupboard. Bundles of cigarette packs were missing. He checked the rows of spirit bottles displayed behind the cash register. There was a gap where an expensive whiskey had been.

He ran out back, but whoever had broken into his store was long gone.

He raised an angry cry into the deserted alley.

"Oh my God! Why can't you leave me alone!"

***

The gang of tearaways arrived laughing and jeering at an overgrown alleyway that bordered the back yards of a row of old houses. The only light came from a streetlamp at the far end of the path that lead back to the road.

They sat down on the damp dirt and leaned against the rotting boards of the wooden fence. The stolen booze was shared around. Cigarettes were lit and the bragging and laughing commenced.

Baggy mocked in an Asian accent.

"Why can't you leave me alone."

He took a swig from the bottle. "I wonder if he delivers?" he joked.

Snake agreed. "Why not? We're regular customers."

"Yeah, and we get five finger discount," replied Bags.

Snake laughed as he reached for the bottle.

"Give it here."

"Brody done OK didn't he." Lloyd said.

Lloyd was always a little protective of Brody.

Snake offered the bottle to the boy.

"Yeah, go on Brody boy, have some."

The young teenager was desperate to fit in.

"Sure. Give it here," he said cockily.

He took a sip, gagged and nearly threw up. The others laughed loudly.

"Come on. Take a proper drink." Baggy said.

"Yeah, here."

Snake pushed the bottle up, forcing Brody to take a huge gulp. Jeering laughter from the others as he coughed and choked.

Still struggling to breath, Brody held the bottle out for someone to take.

That's when the power went out and the whole neighborhood was plunged into darkness.

The sound of glass breaking interrupted the shocked silence as the whiskey bottle slipped from Brody's fingers and smashed on the stoney ground.

"What was that?" Snake said angrily. "Was that the whiskey?"

Baggy and Lloyd let out a moan.

"You smashed the bottle, idiot," Baggy said. "What'd you do that for?"

Snake grabbed Brody.

"That's my whiskey you stupid jackass."

"I, I, thought someone had hold of it, Snake. Honest," Brody whimpered, "I'm sorry."

"I'll make you sorry," Snake threatened. "What are we gonna do for booze?"

"I said I'm sorry. I don't know what to do, Snake," Brody said.

"What about your mom. I hear she likes a drink," Snake sneered. "Maybe there's a bottle or two at your place?"

That hurt. Brody tried not to show it.

The fight was interrupted when Baggy spotted something.

"Hey look! Coming outa that window. It's kinda cool."

The others turned to look.

A brilliant flickering violet light was shining from an upstairs window of the old property right behind the fence.

"Nothing. Just a TV. Idiot," said Snake, still vexed about the booze.

"Oh yeah. A TV," Baggy hastily agreed.

Brody thought differently.

"No, it can't be."

"If Snake says it's a TV, that's what it is - a TV," Lloyd insisted.

Brody may have been the youngest, but he had a mind of his own. It often got him into trouble. His mother thought he was just being stubborn and disagreeable. Her boyfriend, Clayton, said her kid was an ungrateful brat and anyway, all teenagers should just shut the hell up.

Brody wasn't any of those things, he was just wired a little differently.

"But there's no power," insisted Brody.

"Course it's a TV. Who cares anyway?" Baggy said, reaching for a cigarette. "Give me a light someone."

Snake had cooled a little as he lit Baggy's cigarette.

"Hey, kid, who's to say what it is. I say it's just a TV. You say it's not," said Snake. "If it ain't a TV - what is it then?"

Brody gave that some thought.

"Well, it could be... I don't know do I. But there's no power. Look, the whole neighborhood's out. It's kind of weird."

Snake thought about that for a moment and then came to a decision.

"You're so smart. Go get it. Bring back something to prove you're right and I'm wrong. That's your ticket in."

"Ticket in?" Brody said.

"Yeah. Your challenge. If you want to be a full member of the crew."

The booze was beginning to hit Brody.

"Come on, Snake. Don't make me do that. I don't feel well."

"The Snake Crew, Brody. You in or out?" Snake demanded.

"Yeah, go on. Snake Crew boys ain't scared of nothing," bragged Baggy.

Lloyd was a little more sympathetic.

"You can do it, Brody. Easy."

6

The dilapidated fence swayed dangerously under the weight of the thirteen-year-old, as Brody reluctantly struggled to scale it.

Then it sagged inward when Baggy gave Brody a helpful shove. The rotting fence posts started giving way, causing the whole structure to crack and groan as it came to rest against a bush.

Brody teetered at the summit and finally tipped over into the back yard. His fall painfully broken by the same bush that supported the fence panel.

He thrashed his way out and found himself at the bottom of an overgrown wasteland.

He hacked a path through the undergrowth until his cell phone flashlight picked out the decaying timbers of a ramshackle shed propped against the rear of the house.

***

Brody's world spun nauseously from the alcohol as he struggled up the wooden framework. He groped for a foothold on an ancient wisteria that had

7

Across the hallway, Harry used a flashlight as he fussed over his mother, trying to calm her and reassure her that everything was going to be fine.

The sudden darkness had sent her dementia-driven anxiety, rocketing.

"What's happening? Where's Harry?"

"Calm down Mom. It's nothing to worry about. I told you, the power will be back in a moment."

"Harry?"

His mother seemed to recognise her son at last.

"Yes Mom. I'll get your medication. It'll only take a moment," Harry promised. "Please, just stay in bed. Will you do that for me?"

He left the room and called out to Schrodinger sitting just across the hall. "Come on boy. Schrodinger – come." Nothing from the cat. He seemed more interested in something in the workshop.

Harry headed downstairs.

***

In the workshop, Brody tried to make sense of the equipment. He recognised the voltage meter. And there was an oscilloscope; they had one like it at school. This one had a bright green line that was wiggling crazily on the small screen. He couldn't begin to guess why it was doing that.

The closest he could get to putting a name to the rest of it was like getting all the electrical junk from an old TV and radio repair shop, throw in some heavy-duty science apparatus, randomly wire it all together and switch it on to see what happens.

But his gut told him there was meaning and purpose in this particular pile of scrap - whatever that meaning and purpose was.

***

Pinned to the wall were some press cuttings. He played the flashlight over them and noticed a word common to all the headlines. 'Fusion'.

Lost in his curiosity, he moved from one piece of equipment to another. Inevitably, he was drawn back to the glowing glass chamber. This, he figured, was the proof he needed to show Snake.

He pulled at some cables but nothing gave. He tried to move the chamber. With pipes bolted to it there was no way he could shift it and anyway, it was far too heavy to carry.

Aiming his cell phone he took a picture.

Then Brody had an uncanny sense that he wasn't alone. His skin crawled as he turned.

In the doorway, standing silently, he was shocked to see a ghostly apparition, its white hair, pale skin and white gown glowing in the violet light.

She was eerily motionless. A cat was rubbing against her leg.

"Harry? You're late home from school," Harry's mother said.

Brody wanted to run, but the window, his only means of escape, was within the old woman's grasp.

He answered in a terrified whisper.

"I, I'm Ah, Brody. Brody Boyle. Who's Harry?"

Harry was climbing the stairs with a glass of water and the medication. He was surprised to see his mother standing in the doorway of his workshop, her back to him.

"Mom! Come on. I've got your tablets."

He gently manoeuvred her back to her room, tucked the blankets around her and handed her a pill and the glass of water.

"I spoke to Harry," she said. "He's back home from school." It was said with absolute certainty as she swallowed the medication.

"Now you know you shouldn't be in my lab, Mom. It's dangerous, and well, just stay in your bedroom."

Across the hall, Brody had stopped to listen to the conversation.

"But Harry'll be needing his dinner. He gets hungry after school. His sister should start preparing the vegetables. I'll be down in a minute."

Harry was already leaving the room. "I'll tell her, but promise me you'll stay in bed."

He stopped at the doorway.

"The lights will be back on shortly, Mom," he said to reassure her.

He pulled the door gently closed.

Realising he was about to be discovered, Brody bolted for the window.

Harry was shocked to see the youngster flit past the open doorway.

"Hey! You! What the hell?!"

Brody clambered on to the table as he made a break for the open window, knocking tools and equipment to the floor.

Harry bounded into the room enraged at the brazen intrusion but hesitated at the sound of his mother's voice.

"Is that you Harry? Maybe I'll go put dinner on."

Conflicted, Harry urged his mother to stay in bed.

Still giddy from alcohol, Brody reached out to steady himself against the wall. It took a moment for the dizziness to pass. He didn't notice the press cutting caught in his fingers as he took his hand away.

Harry lunged for the thief.

"What have you stolen? Give it here."

Brody easily dodged the old man, but his vision blurred momentarily just as he stepped through the window. The sudden disorientation made him slip as he struggled to get a foothold on the vine.

Harry's mother worried about needing to set the dinner table.

Harry looked over to her.

"No, stay in your bedroom Mom."

Then, to the intruder, as the boy began to climb down.

"I know you, you and your thieving friends. I'll call the police."

In the hallway, Harry's mother was fumbling in the dark with one foot on the treacherous staircase.

"I'll go downstairs and do it myself."

Panic stricken, Harry turned from Brody and rushed to help his mother.

***

Outside, Brody missed his grip, tumbled out of the wisteria and landed heavily in the shrubbery.

He got unsteadily to his feet. Swayed a little. Then another spell of nausea caused him to bend over and projectile vomit into the flower bed.

He had never felt so ill, what with the cold sweat and the headache. It was worse than the food poisoning that had kept him off school for a few days last year.

One thing was certain. He wasn't going to touch that horrible whiskey stuff ever again. No sir. His drinking days were over.

His hand went to wipe his mouth.

It was then he noticed the torn press cutting. Focusing on the text made him nauseous again so he shoved it in his pocket. The cat watched from the window as he took off down the yard, back to the fence.

He tumbled into the alley just as the street light flickered back on. The first thing that was clear when he checked up and down the lane, it seemed the Snake Crew, his so-called friends – his family – couldn't be bothered to wait.

They had taken off and abandoned him.

8

He made his way home through bleak, deserted streets. Too cold, tired and hungry to notice a police car approaching from behind. The strobing blue and red lights were what finally got his attention.

Brody turned to look and froze as two officers got out. He recognised one of them.

Deputy Dave Fiennes, six feet of fresh southern charm in his cowboy hat, and a reputation as a tough but fair cop. He was born in the town some thirty-eight years ago and never had an itch to settle anywhere else.

As far as he was concerned, from the day he enlisted and put the uniform on, his job was to serve and protect his family, his friends, citizens, businesses and visitors. In fact, the whole fly-blown neighborhood from one end of Jorden County to the other. And that's about as far as his ambition went.

Well, almost; there was one other personal ambition that, up until now, he'd managed to keep private. But that was work that was still very much in progress.

"Hey Brody. It's pretty late. What's up?" Officer Fiennes asked.

Brody gave the time-worn, sullen, teenage response that would make Bart Simpson proud.

"Nothing."

The second officer, a pimply new recruit, piped up. "You seen your pals McKay or Marchant?"

Then to Fiennes, "Who's that other one?"

"Lloyd Ferris," Fiennes said. "Some stuff was taken from a store earlier. You know anything about that, Brody?"

Brody shook his head sulkily.

"Funny, 'cause the owner remembers a kid dressed like you. Your age," the recruit pressed.

He waited for a response but got nothing.

Officer Fiennes added some detail.

"Says you may have stolen something while the shop was being robbed out back."

The recruit sneered an alternative scenario.

"Na, you were distracting him while the shop was being robbed by your pals. Ain't that right?"

"Got nothing to do with me. I'm just going home."

The recruit fancied himself as some kind of local, NCIS investigator.

"Why, where've you been, out this late?"

"I needed a walk. To get out the house."

This brought a sympathetic response from Fiennes.

"You still got problems at home, Brody?"

A long pause. Brody was reluctant to talk about it.

"Come on. Get in. We'll take you home."

The recruit objected.

"We're not a taxi service. He can walk."

Fiennes was already walking the boy to the car.

"We can't let him walk the streets. You got anything better to do?"

"Or maybe you got a thing for his mother." A snarky shot from the recruit.

"Well, that's between me and her."

Officer Dave Fiennes' other ambition was still a state secret and it would stay that way until he was good and ready.

9

The front door opened quietly as Brody slipped into the shabby hallway. Stairs were ahead. The door to the lounge open.

Softly, as careful as anyone could be who had seen moments like this explode into sudden violence, he snuck into the lounge.

The TV was on but his mother, Rachel, and her boyfriend, Clayton, were comatose on the couch. On the coffee table, scattered amongst bottles of cheap wine and beer, were the remains of a Chinese take-out.

He tip-toed across and checked for any leftovers. The chicken was gone but there was a handful of rice at the bottom of a container.

It wasn't much but he was starving. He hadn't eaten since school lunch and was already salivating at the thought of the pathetic banquet.

He took another look at the couch. No sign of life. His hands shook a little as he carefully lifted the container from amongst the bottles.

Disaster. The box knocked one of the bottles with a muted clink. It started to topple. He caught it with his other hand and gently let it settle back on the table.

He checked again for signs of life. Took a breath, and snuck back out into the hallway.

He was two steps up when a hand grabbed him roughly from behind.

"You stealing my food you thieving ingrate?"

The boyfriend, drunk and aggressive as usual, dragged Brody back down to the hallway and tried to wrench the box from his hand.

The boy hung on to the box as though his life depended on it. That handful of rice was going upstairs to his room one way or another.

"Gimme that or so help me, I'll knock you from here to the back end of next Friday."

He raised his hand just as Brody's mother, staggered into the hallway.

"Leave him alone, Clayton."

She grabbed her boyfriend's arm in mid-swing, dragging her with it. It failed to connect with its target, but smacked the rice out of Brody's grasp, and scattered across the floor.

Experience had taught Rachel to be wary of her boyfriend's violent temper.

She shouted a warning.

"Get to bed Brody. Now!"

"No you don't. Clear this mess up, you useless waste of space." Clayton shouted.

"I'll do it," Rachel said. "Go to bed Brody."

Clayton pushed her away. She landed heavily against the front door and slid drunkenly to the floor.

The bully leaned in aggressively to Brody

"CLEAN - IT - UP."

The kid did as he was told. Cowering like an abused puppy, he went to the kitchen to find something to clean the mess.

"Leave him alone. You're not his father. You've got no right."

The boyfriend turned to Rachel. His face red with alcohol and rage.

"Are you disrespecting me? No wonder your kid's out of control," he shouted. "Shut it!"

"Yeah, well he doesn't need you shouting at him."

The bully's hand went to his belt.

"I said shut your pie hole - or so help me."

The boy returned with a pan and brush and started sweeping. Clayton watched for a moment then boredom set in. He lost interest, slouched into the living room, dropped on to the couch and passed out.

Brody's mother crawled over and took the pan and brush from her son.

"I'll do it. Go to bed," she whispered.

"No Mom, it's OK."

She tugged on the brush and nodded her head to the floor above.

***

An unmade bed filled most of the small room where Brody slept. The walls were buried behind posters of movies and bands. A table lamp was squeezed next to an old PC on a small table. All three salvaged from thrift shops.

Brody fell onto the bed hungry and exhausted. He turned to face the ceiling and just managed to convert a small sob of despair into a grimace of anger.

10

In the school canteen the usual noisy, chaotic chatter of students added to the industrial clatter of trays, cutlery and crockery.

Brody inched along with the other students in the lunch line. He slid his tray down the stainless-steel rail, offering his plate up to each assistant as he went.

Lloyd barged in behind him.

"Where were you this morning? Late night?" he said with a smirk.

Brody shrugged.

Lloyd filled his plate while he continued to goad his friend.

"You didn't miss much. History. What more do I need to know? I mean, me and the brothers, we were oppressed. It's just tragic."

"You didn't wait," Brody said sullenly.

He scanned the busy hall looking for an empty table. One became free nearby. He had to push the abandoned plates to one side to make room for his tray.

Lloyd followed and found a scrap of space for his own plate. He quickly took a few hungry mouthfuls before getting down to the issue of the dirty plates.

"Lazy losers s'posed to clear their stuff. Look at this mess."

With his belly complaining, Brody had stuffed his face like a scavenger. All he could manage was a shrug of agreement.

***

They ate in silence for a few more mouthfuls before Brody was ready to talk.

"Cops stopped me last night. Asked about you."

"They can't prove nothing," Lloyd said, his mouth loaded with potatoes. "You're the only one he saw. Did you take anything?

Brody shrugged again.

"Right, so you're in the clear and so are we. Stay cool. Anyway, so, what happened in that house? Did you get anything?"

"Well, it wasn't a TV," Brody declared. "I said it wasn't, didn't I."

"Yeah, but Snake wanted proof, you know, if you want to join the crew."

"It was weird, Lloyd. There was this, like, flickering light in a glass bottle and loads of equipment. You know, like in a science lab. And a noise – like some kind of machine."

Lloyd put on a spooky voice and did jazz hands.

"What, like a time machine, Brody? A doorway to another planet? An alien life force?"

"I don't know," he scooped another mouthful.

It was a little while before he spoke again.

"I took a picture."

He reached for his phone and thumbed his way to the photo. The violet light was bright but blurry against a dark and indistinct background.

Lloyd shrugged indifferently.

"So - what? It's just an LED."

Brody brightened a little.

"But, if the electricity was off, where's it getting the power?

"Batteries," his friend said emphatically.

Lloyd swallowed the last mouthful.

"I'm outa here."

He got up and started to walk away.

"You'll never guess who it was," said Brody. "In that house."

Lloyd turned and waited.

Brody said, "Old Figgy."

His friend shot back cynically.

"What, old Figgy's opened a portal to the gates of hell?"

As Brody reached for his dessert.

"Yeah. In his bedroom!"

11

A small room next to the school science lab was Harry Figg's day-time domain. As the lab assistant to the school science classes, his job was to prepare and set out the equipment used for lessons.

He was seated at his bench as still as a statue. Only Harry's eyes moved as they followed something with total concentration.

His hand was raised in the air, a rolled-up magazine in his fist. The target just needed to choose a place to land.

Like a lizard watching his prey, it was all over in a nano-second. The journal slammed down on the fly that had been irritating the hell out of him for the past twenty minutes.

Satisfied, he leaned back in his chair, unrolled the periodical, wiped away the remains of the insect and browsed the pages.

The magazine's cover title boasted, 'Scientific Horizons'. The headline: 'Fusion – An Unattainable Dream?'.

Harry was deeply engrossed when science teacher Penny Wallace entered and she was in a hurry.

"Harry, I need the water electrolysis experiment for two o'clock?"

Harry grudgingly got out of his chair, eyes still glued to the page. He waved an acknowledgment in her direction.

Penny checked her watch.

"Ten minutes?"

A grunt from Harry as she ducked back out. Harry began searching along the cluttered shelves, muttering to himself.

"Batteries."

***

It was a typical science classroom with rows of lab benches facing a whiteboard and a large TV screen.

The room was already filling with students noisily taking their places – four to a bench. On the walls were posters for the school Annual Science Fair. 'Students are encouraged to get involved', it appealed hopefully.

Harry Figg was pushing a cart taking batteries, glass flasks and other items to each work bench.

Some of the students whispered cruel jokes about him to each other as he went by. It's a truth as old as time; the oddball, the one that's different – *not one of us* – the easy target for school bullies.

Harry knew. He pretended not to notice.

Brody entered gloomily with his hands deep in his pockets and sauntered over to a bench.

His fingers wrapped around something that felt like paper. Withdrawing his hand, he saw it was the crumpled newspaper cutting from the night before. Just looking at it brought back memories of the nausea and the vomiting. He could almost smell the whiskey.

He placed the torn fragment on the bench and began ironing it flat with the palm of his hand.

Then he leaned in to read it.

The squeaky wheel of Harry's cart made him look up. He was heading his way. Alarmed, he dropped down behind the bench and pretended to tie the lace of his trainer.

Harry began placing equipment on the work surface, one set of instruments and chemicals between two. The scrap of paper caught his eye. He instantly recognised it.

Leaning over the bench, he looked down and locked eyes with the kid.

"Oh, hi Mr. Figg," Brody said sheepishly.

Harry said nothing. He just brandished the press cutting for Brody to see.

The boy reacted with brazen innocence.

"What are we doing today then Mr. Figg?"

Harry raised an eyebrow, placed the cutting back on the table and moved on.

Lloyd arrived and took his place next to Brody. He'd seen the confrontation between Harry and his friend.

"Do you think old Figgy recognised you?"

"Of course he did."

"What did he say?"

"He didn't say nothing."

"What's with the newspaper cutting?" Lloyd asked.

"Nothing. Just something I took from his house."

On the next bench a girl had been watching Brody. He caught her looking. She turned away quickly. They were both embarrassed.

"Oh, hi Laura," Brody muttered awkwardly.

Her friend, Stacey, sniggered and nudged Laura. Laura reddened and made a play of getting her stuff ready for the lesson.

***

At the front of the class the teacher, Penny Wallace, attempted to calm the room and get the lesson started.

"Right. OK. Settle down. STUDENTS!" She finally got a reaction. "Alright."

On the whiteboard she inked out a heading, saying the words out loud, syllable by syllable.

"Wa - ter - elec - trol - y – sis," she underlined it and turned to the students.

"Water electrolysis. Anyone?"

Silence at last descended in the room. The students look to each other for clues. She looked across and spotted Brody reading the press cutting.

"How about you Brody Boyle?"

He looked up, confused.

"Sorry miss? What?"

Laughter from the other kids as Penny walked over. Nobody wants to be picked on.

Lloyd ducked away.

"Here she comes," he whispered.

"Water electrolysis," Penny said.

She pointed to the whiteboard. "Any idea what that is?"

While Brody was pondering the question, she looked at the press cutting, picked it up and spent a moment reading it.

Brody closed his eyes and waited for the hell he was sure was about to break loose.

But Penny Wallace didn't have a mean bone in her body.

"Well, I'll grant you one thing Brody, this is a science lesson. But don't you think nuclear fusion is a little advanced for ninth grade?"

"I don't know miss. I don't know what it is. I was just... you know..."

"Not paying attention? Was that what you were doing?"

She replaced the press cutting and tapped it as she walked away.

"Save it for later."

She had nearly reached the whiteboard at the front of class when Brody blurted out that it was something about oxygen and something else - H2O?

The teacher turned in surprise.

"Sorry?"

"That thing," he pointed to the whiteboard. "Is it about oxygen? And hyd -hyder - hydrogen?"

Penny couldn't hide her astonishment.

"Hydrogen and oxygen? Yes. Anything else?"

She turned to the rest of the class.

"Anybody?"

She walked to whiteboard and tapped the words.

"OK, today, unlike Brody's nuclear fusion, we're going to unhitch some atoms. Separate water molecules into oxygen and hydrogen atoms."

She paused for dramatic effect.

"Now, fill your flasks with water and then add a handful of salt."

The room become busy as students started to prepare the experiment.

12

In a small, windowless interview room, furnished with a metal table and three chairs, powder was being poured into a glass tumbler of water.

Police officer Alison Renfrew was sitting in one of the chairs nursing a black eye. She took a good swallow of the pain killer, which according to the packet on the table was the fastest working anti-inflammatory you can buy across the counter without a prescription.

Slumped in the chair opposite was Brody's mother, Rachel.

The officer spoke at last.

"Where's your son - Brody?"

"He's at school."

"You sure about that, Rachel?" Renfrew asked. "They found him wandering the streets late last night."

"I don't know anything about that. He's at school. He's a good boy."

"Yes, well, some of the kids he hangs around with aren't so good, are they?"

Rachel groaned and rested her head on her arms, folded on the table.

"Take me home."

Renfrew leaned forward to speak. There was concern in her voice.

"Look, Mrs Boyle, ah, Rachel - we're worried about Brody. We may have to bring in Social Services."

This was the threat that had hung over Brody's mother since her husband abandoned them three years ago.

"No, no, don't do that. They'll take my boy. Just get me home," Rachel started sobbing. "Brody needs me. I've got to cook his supper."

"Well, that boyfriend of yours will be cooling his heels in a cell overnight," Renfrew said, rubbing her eye. "He's got a hell of a temper. That's another bar that's got Clayton's face on the 'Stay Away' flyer."

Clayton was going for a record-breaking, full house of bars he'd been banned from in the town and quite a few across the county.

"It's the drink makes him crazy," Rachel said feebly.

Renfrew shook her head sadly.

"I'll see about getting you home."

She got up and left the room.

13

Penny had to raise her voice. "... and I need a page with diagrams and detailed explanation on my desk in the morning. That includes you, Morris - You too, Lloyd," she instructed.

A bell rang throughout the school and the lesson came to an end. The students were already getting restless and noisy.
She pointed to the Science Fair poster.
"Don't forget to enter something for the Science Fair. And please put some thought into it this time, yes? Let's get spectacular!" she added with desperate enthusiasm.

Penny Wallace's pet project was under threat. The last few years had seen it reduced to poor attendance and slapdash contributions from a largely disinterested student population. She needed this year's Science Fair to do better. A lot better.

She shuffled some paperwork on her desk then remembered something.

"Brody Boyle."

Brody was already heading out into the corridor with Lloyd. He heard his name but pretended not to notice.

"Brody! A moment." Penny called out a little louder.

He stopped and mooched sullenly over to the science teacher.

"Yes miss?"

"I need you to help Mr. Figg with the equipment."

Catastrophe. This was not something he wanted to hear.

"But Miss Wallace!" he gulped.

"Not now, Brody," she said dismissively. "Give Mr. Figg a hand."

She followed the other students out of the room and left Brody alone with Harry.

***

Harry was over on the other side of the class room clearing equipment from the tables to his cart. He didn't appear to have noticed the boy.

Brody didn't move but shoved his hands in his pockets and eyed Harry suspiciously.

A moment passed.

"What's that light then?" Brody said morosely.

Harry continued working as he replied.

"Why do you care?"

Brody had to think about that for a moment. *Why did he care?* His answer surprised even a young cynic like Brody, because he knew it was true.

"I was just, you know – curious?"

Harry nodded his head. That was the right answer.

"It's a star in a jar."

"I'm not stupid." the boy grumbled.

Harry stopped what he was doing and looked up.

"You broke into my house. I should call the police."

"Go on then," Brody challenged.

Silence…

"Nuclear fusion. Read the press cutting you stole."

"I've read it. It's science." He said *science* as though it was some kind of magical incantation.

Harry stifled his amusement.

"Actually, it's quantum mechanics."

Another silence broken by the squeaky wheel as Harry pushed the cart to another bench.

"Aren't you supposed to be helping?"

After a pause Brody reluctantly walked over and offered sullen help.

"The power was out but that thing was still working."

"Yes, I've got a power supply problem." Harry said.

Brody took one of the batteries from the bench and held it thoughtfully for a moment, before placing it on the cart.

"My friend Lloyd says it runs on batteries, 'cos otherwise how could it work?"

"What do you think Brody?" Harry wasn't going to make it easy for the teenager.

"That setup in your room, it's like something out of science fiction."

Harry stopped and looked at Brody.

"Well, it's not science fiction."

"What is it then?" he said defiantly.

Harry took the last of the batteries from the boy and placed them on the cart.

"It's for me to know and you to find out."

He walked off, rolling the cart back to the annex. Brody watched as the door closed.

His curiosity had just become an itch he needed to scratch.

14

"Hi Snake. Baggs." Brody called out as he ambled down main street towards his Snake Crew pals.

They turned their backs and froze him out.

It was mid-afternoon. School was over for the day and like most students, they were in town, free and looking for something interesting to do and mischief to make.

Snake, Baggy and Lloyd were chatting to a group of girls and trying their best to look cool and mature. The vapes were the go-to shortcut to achieve the full adult look. That and the tats two of the girls were already cooing over.

What Snake and Baggy didn't want was to have some uncool thirteen-year-old standing next to them like a kid brother.

While two of the girls had bought the boys corny sales pitch, the other one, Laura, wanted to move on. That was until she saw Brody approaching.

Only Lloyd acknowledged him with a guilty nod as he arrived.

Laura was about the same age as Brody, maybe a few months older. Dark hair cut short and practical. She had a permanent look of amusement on her face which Brody found attractive though he couldn't explain why if you asked him. And she came across as a little more mature than him, as all girls seemed to at that age.

She had one other attractive trait – she was shy but definitely interested in Brody.

"You didn't make it to school this morning." Laura said, getting the conversation started.

Brody tried to play it cool to impress his older friends.

"Yeah, well, I was busy wasn't I."

"Doing what?"

"Oh, you know." Then he remembered what Harry Figg had said. "Anyway, that's for me to know and you to find out."

"I was only asking, Brody. You don't have to be mean."

Brody blushed at the truth of her rebuke.

***

The Snake Crew boys swaggered away with the other two girls, laughing and teasing.

Uninvited, Brody followed behind and flicked his head to Laura in a mute invitation for her to join him. She shook her head stubbornly and stayed put.

It was as though she had lassoed him. He jerked to a stop and watched his friends, weighing his options as they walked away. A defining moment.

He walked back to Laura.

"Well? What *do* you want to do?" He asked.

Laura tested him, "You're not going with your friends, Brody?"

He turned to look at his pals retreating down the sidewalk, playing up to the girls, laughing and joking. Jealous of their bravado and confidence.

He took a deep breath, stuffed his hands in his pockets and shrugged.

"Let's get a smoothie," Laura suggested.

"I don't want a smoothie."

"What do you like then?"

"Nothing."

After another pause.

"I'm buying," she said.

"OK, that's cool."

They walked over to the nearby coffee house.

15

The Jake O Bean was a cosy Mom and Pop coffee and shake bar where all the kids hung out. Jake, the owner, sat at his usual spot by the register near the door reading the sports pages.

Jake didn't mind the kids, it could get noisy sometimes, but they respected him and paid their bills. He had a bowl of change he dipped into if they came up short occasionally.

***

Brody and Laura strolled in and gave Jake the usual greeting.

"Hey Jake."

They walked past Roberts and Torres who were sitting opposite each other deep in conversation on the red benches of a booth by the window.

Check in to a coffee house or diner across America, no matter how remote, from the Atlantic to the Pacific, you'll find the seats are covered in classic red leatherette. The Jake O Bean was no exception.

Roberts hailed the waiter.

"Hey kid! Some refills here."

He turned to Torres. "So, what you thinking? We grab this thing and hightail it out of here? We don't want to be in this dump any longer than we have to."

"Easy boy. We don't really know what we're up against, or what this thing looks like. If it's anything like the machine they've got back at The Corporation labs, it could be huge.

The young server, looked about nineteen, arrived with the refills. His face sported Māori tattoo graphics, a nose ring and on his shirt, a badge identifying him as "Steve". He proceeded to refill the cups.

Roberts watched Steve while he spoke to Torres.

"Who is this guy, Harry Figg? What's he doing in a town like this? If he's such a genius, shouldn't he be working at NASA or something?

Upon hearing the name, Steve stopped pouring the coffee and interrupted the conversation.

"You talking about old Figgy?"

A pause as the two spies did a quick reset.

"Old Figgy? You know this man?" asked Torres.

"Sure, if it's the same old guy I know."

Roberts wanted to be sure.

"We're talking about Harry Figg?"

Steve spoke with a cocky confidence, "He's just some old weird guy from school. A Janitor or something."

The waiter made a rotating sign with his finger to his head.

"Not playing with a full deck. I mean the guy still lives with his mother for Christ's sake."

He went back to the business of pouring coffee.

Torres said, "So, he works at the local high school?"

"I just said that didn't I?"

He lost interest, turned and sauntered over to some girls sitting at another booth.

"You're kidding, right, Torres? A janitor?"

He tried to hide an 'I told you so' smirk.

"You never saw the movie, 'Good Will Hunting'? You've got a mind like a mouse trap, Roberts: It snaps shut at the first sniff of cheese."

16

In Brody's bedroom, the press cutting lay on the desk next to the PC he was using to search for info on fusion reactors.

What he found was a confusing mess of complex science and baffling words.

His mother entered, subdued and thoughtful. Brody didn't seem to notice and anyway, he didn't take his eyes off of the screen.

"I've been calling you," she said.

"Didn't hear Mom," his eyes still scanning the results of his online research.

"Well, your dinner's getting cold."

"Be down."

Rachel wanted to show she cared about her son's interests. She wanted to be part of it.

"What are you doing, Brody? What's all that stuff you're looking at?" she said, trying to be a good mom. A mother her son could be proud of.

"Nothing, Mom."

The indifference cut her like a knife.

After a pause she said.
"Ok - well - your dinners getting cold..."

She left quietly. He didn't notice.

Shortly after he found an image that interested him. He reached for his phone and browsed to the picture he'd taken in Harry's workshop. He held it up to the screen for comparison.
They were similar.

He read the accompanying text to himself.
"Fusion can produce vast amounts of clean energy that could replace fossil fuels. But scientists haven't solved the problem of how to contain the hot plasma gases".
He pinned the press cutting to the wall.
"So, what's old Figgy got in his back room?" he wondered.

***

Brody and his mom were sitting at the table in the living room. Dinner of hot dog fried rice was coming to an end. The TV in the corner was on. The sound low.
Mom drank water while Brody shoved in a final hungry mouthful. He sensed something had changed.

"It's good Mom. We haven't had this in a long while."

Rachel was pleased. She played it simple.

"Just scraped together what we could afford. Leftovers mainly."

"Bit fancy, sitting at the table?"

"Yes, well, things are going to change round here, Brody."

"I like it better when your boyfriend's not around."

Nothing from his mother. She couldn't fix the past. Maybe she could do something about the future.

Brody felt his phone vibrate. He took it from his pocket and found an incoming message from Laura.

"Hello. What r u doing?"

"Not much. U?"

"I'm bored"

A pause as Brody considered what to type next.

"Brody. You still there?"

Laura seemed keen.

Brody typed.

"Want to see a star in a jar?"

17

Brody jumped on his bike and rode like the wind, heading for the Jake O Bean - and Laura. His heart pounded and not just because he was pumping the peddles so hard.

The Jake O was two doors away from a popular liquor store. Brody arrived, out of breath and eager to see Laura. But instead he was surprised to find Snake and Baggy loitering outside.

"Hey, Brody boy. Good timing," said Snake McKay.

"Why, what's up?" Brody asked innocently.

Snake ignored him and turned to Baggy.

"Go! Baggsy."

Baggy pulled the hoody over his head and stormed into the liquor store.

"I'm going to need those wheels, Brodeo."

He grabbed the bike, pushed Brody off and climbed on, setting the pedals ready for a quick getaway.

"No Snake! I need my bike." He was desperate.

He grabbed the handlebars and tried pulling and wriggling it to free it from Snake's grip, but Snake pushed him hard in the chest, making Brody stagger back.

"I told you. I need the bike. OK, kid?" Snake said.

There was shouting and commotion from inside the liquor store. Then Baggy ran out carrying a couple of bottles.

He was actually laughing.

"Go Snake! DoorDash - no cash."

Snake was already starting to cycle off as Baggy leaped onto the panier rack. The extra weight made the mud guard rub on the rear tyre so that it buzzed noisily as they weaved and wobbled down the sidewalk.

The store owner burst out into the street, his cell phone in his hand, hollering and cussing.

"I got the police coming. They're gonna throw you in jail you freakin' trouble-makers."

It was Snake Crew business but Brody didn't want anything to do with it. He took off like an elite runner in a hundred-metre sprint, across the road and into a nearby alleyway.

***

Laura arrived outside the coffee house just as law enforcement showed up, lights strobing.

Larry, the liquor store owner, angrily confronted one of the officers as she stepped out of the car.

"Bout time you did something 'bout those kids, Alison. They hit my store so often I should be on their Christmas card list."

Officer Alison Renfrew agreed, "Yeah, and they're on our shit list, Larry. You mentioned tattoos? Sounds like that one-kid-crimewave, Snake McKay or his side-kick, Marchant." She said as she crossed the sidewalk to the store.

"You think?" Larry said sardonically.

Inside the scene of the crime everything looked much as she expected – the thieves run in grab a couple of bottles and run out.

"That video camera attached to anything, Larry?"

Larry looked up to the corner where the old CCTV camera was installed.

"Yeah, well I've been meaning to get that fixed," he said sheepishly.

Alison nodded, "I suppose if he was wearing a hoody or a cap, we couldn't ID him anyway."

She browsed around trying to look professional. She planned to get a detective ticket if the chief supported her like he said he would.

She reached for a bottle of Napa Valley's cheapest red.

"Might as well shop while I'm here." She put a ten-dollar bill on the counter.

Larry rang up eight dollars thirty-five cents, gave her change and slipped the bottle into a bag.

"You get friends and family discount, Alison."

"Much obliged as always," she said as she stepped back out into the street.

"Look, a bit of advice Larry," she added. "Get that camera fixed, or you might as well stop paying your insurance. You know they won't pay out if they see it's not working don't you."

Larry stopped at the door.

"Sure thing. I'm on it. Now what about those kids?"

Renfrew climbed into her car.

"Yeah, well, don't worry. We'll catch 'em, Larry."

Laura watched as the police cruiser drove away, decided Brody wasn't going to turn up, turned her bike around and cycled off.

Brody sank despondently to the ground, his back against the wall. He ducked as the police car drove past, lights flashing. Then he felt a buzz as his cell vibrated. It was a message from Laura.

"Never speak to me again, Brody Boyle."

18

As an older person who was starting to notice the pain of arthritis in his joints, squeezing under the work bench was a time-consuming activity that required both planning and resolve.

And that's where Harry was, working on a hard-to-reach component, when he heard a soft knock on the front door.

He ignored it.

The sound came again, a little louder.

Harry was not a particularly sociable person. He didn't like visitors. Especially at night.

He muttered as he worked.

"Just go away!"

He waited a moment. Seemed like the visitor had given up. The last bolt just needed a little more tightening, which he started to do when the door got rapped again - much louder.

A feeble voice from across the hall.

"There's someone at the door, Harry."

"Yeah, I heard it Mom. Jeez - I'm coming for pity's sake."

Irritated, he wiggled his way out from under the bench and headed downstairs. Whoever it was, he was going to give them a piece of his mind – making a nuisance at this time of night. Goodness knows if he'll ever get his mother calmed down again.

As he opened the door he hissed, "Keep it down."

But was surprised to find Brody standing there.

"You! What do you want?"

He checked up and down the street.

"Where are your friends? Why can't you kids just leave me alone."

He started to close the door but Brody appealed to him.

"It's not like that Mr. Figg. I'm on my own."

Harry eyed him suspiciously, still watching the street. "Well, what do you want?"

"You said it was for me to find out," the boy said. "You know - the star in a jar? Well, here I am."

Harry considered this for a moment. He turned and started back upstairs.

"Come on then. Close the door - quietly!" As an afterthought he added, "And mind the stair carpet."

A cat slipped through the gap of the closing door and followed Brody as he climbed the stairs to Harry's workshop.

His jaw dropped open in astonishment at the change. The experiment had grown. More pipes, power cables and a sphere surrounded by coils of copper windings. He'd seen something similar in pictures of old radial aero engines, like the ones they had on those vintage biplanes from the first world war.

Harry explained with a childlike enthusiasm; it was rare to have an audience.

"My original design worked but consumed more power than it produced and the neutrino count was very low, maybe because the deuterium wasn't pure enough. I've had to increase the voltage substantially to get more hydrogen atoms to fuse into helium but the Variac kept burning out…"

His passion spluttered to a standstill when he saw Brody's total incomprehension.

"Yes - well. This system upgrade should improve the performance and eventually produce abundant, carbon-free energy."

"What?" said Brody, still none the wiser.

"The fusion reactor. It's how all electricity will be produced in the future. Why, what did you think it was?"

After a thoughtful pause, Brody pointed to the press cuttings pinned to the wall.

"A fusion reactor? But everyone says it's impossible. Nobody's done it yet, have they?"

"Oh, the Tokamacs are working alright," Harry enthused. "They've had one running for nearly a full second. And the French have one that can do a bit better but it needs to reach temperatures ten times hotter than the core of the sun."

"Well, how come you've got one in your bedroom?" Brody said, "Isn't it dangerous?"

Harry climbed back under the bench.

"First of all, this isn't a bedroom – it's a laboratory."

This was an important distinction for Harry. "And second of all, this one is different. It's a hybrid. I came up with another way to achieve fusion at lower temperatures but it still needs a lot of power."

Brody noticed the fat cable snaking out of the room through a hole in the wall.

"What's with the cable?"

"It's wired into the four-phase electricity supply, which, I'll be honest with you, is a bit unreliable," he said, completely understating the problem.

Harry crawled back out from under the bench, sat in his old office chair and started flicking switches and adjusting controls. As he did, a low hum began to increase in volume.

"OK. Uh, maybe you'd better step back a little, Brody. This thing can pump out a few x-rays even though its shielded. Don't worry, the neutrinos will just pass right through you though."

Alarmed, Brody shuffled over to the window. The humming increased and then a pump started up.

"I've replaced the old vacuum pump with this industrial one. It could suck the gas out of a Zeppelin in sixty seconds."

Harry slowly twisted the large, gnarled knob on a huge mains supply transformer. Through a glass porthole in the sphere at the centre of the apparatus a violet light started flickering. Needles on dials began to move towards the far end of their scales.

Brody sniffed. There was a definite odour of something electrical that he couldn't place.

The old inventor noticed it too.

"Smell that? The air is being ionised. It's a byproduct of the fusion process."

Harry took a hand-held device and held it at various places over the equipment. It clicked rapidly. He nodded with satisfaction and gave the power knob another nudge.

The room light flickered and blinked out causing Harry to get up and look out of the window.

The neighborhood was in darkness.

"Yeah, that's a problem."

"So, the power is out but the thing's still running?" Brody wondered.

"Yes, that's the beauty of my design. It's making enough energy to power itself. No one else has achieved that.

Brody thought Harry should tell someone about his invention.

"I know what they call me. Old Figgy. The crazy old science class assistant," Harry said with a creditable lack of self-pity. "Why would the likes of MIT or University of California take me seriously?"

"But look. Here's the proof."

Harry checked the different settings on the oscilloscope and then reached for some glasses that looked like swimming goggles, the type with two round darkened lenses. He held them to his eyes as he peered through the porthole to observe the brilliant atomic reaction held in place inside the chamber by whatever quantum magic this strange man had conjured up.

Satisfied, he put the glasses to one side.

"Anyway, it's not ready. There seems to be a barrier that prevents higher energies. I think maybe it's the scale. If I reveal my idea now, someone will solve that problem and claim the invention as their own."

A cry from another room interrupted him.

"Harry! Harry!"

Schrodinger had been curled up under the bench, but sprang to attention at the sound of her voice.

"Coming Mom. Look, you better go. Just let yourself out," he said. "Look, you can come back again - if you want to."

The invitation pleased Brody.

"Totally. I'd like that."

***

The neighborhood was in darkness as Brody pulled the front door closed. He walked up the weed-strewn stone path to the road.

As he turned onto the sidewalk, he noticed an SUV parked opposite. The people inside were faintly visible. Brody had a strong suspicion they were looking at him. Maybe even watching Harry's house. But it was late and he needed to get home.

Roberts and Torres faces were lit by the glow from the device in Torres' hand.

She panned the Geiger counter back and forth causing the click count to rise noisily every time it swept past Harry's house.

"Let's check around the back," she said.

In the alley behind the house, the two spies were silhouetted against the violet light streaming out of the second-floor window. The Geiger counter was clicking manically, like a prairie full of crickets.

Roberts still wasn't convinced.

"Could be anything. Like a fusor maybe. Amateur stuff."

Torres shook her head with contempt.

"Roberts, you're priceless."

19

The next day, Lloyd rode his bike through town like a bat with its tail on fire.

Earlier, Brody had called and begged him to meet at the Jake O Bean. He had a couple of important things on his mind.

Maybe Lloyd could help.

***

Brody was on his own in a booth. He'd been sitting there for a while, hoping to catch sight of Laura. He needed to fix things with her. Well, she hadn't turned up yet.

At last Lloyd arrived nodding a hello to Steve. He mooched down the aisle, gave a fist bump to someone he knew, and shuffled onto the bench across from Brody.

"What's up?" Lloyd asked.

"You seen Snake?" Brody wondered.

"No, but Snake and Baggy are laying low. I think they're in trouble."

"Yeah, they jacked some booze from the liquor store a couple of doors down, last night."

Waiter Steve arrived at their table to take an order.

"You kids buying or are we just wet nursing you till your mothers get here?"

"You're an asshole Steve. No, wait, a minute - assholes are useful."

Steve indicated the door with his thumb.

"There's the door. I need the table."

"Gimme a shake." Lloyd said.

Steve looked expectantly at Brody.

"No, I'm good."

"He'll have a shake too."

Brody's threadbare economic situation wasn't a secret.

"You particular about flavours?" Steve ventured.

Lloyd said, "Surprise us, Steve."

Brody was a little more specific, "Chocolate and cashew?"

While all this was going on, Laura entered with a couple of friends. She made a big thing about ignoring Brody, her head turned away and a sudden laugh to show how much fun she and the girls were having – without Brody.

But she made a big fuss of Steve, squeezing past intimately in the narrow space.

"Hey Steve, love the cool tattoo. I bet you wouldn't let a girl down, not like some losers I know."

"Coffee's on me Laura. Catch you in a minute."

He practically strutted like a preening matador. The very cute Laura coming on to him was something he wanted everyone in the Jake O to notice.

Laura gave Brody a sniffy look and walked past.

If she was trying to make a point, it was message received and understood, as far as Brody was concerned.

Hostile located. Missile launched. Target devastated.

"What was that all about?" Lloyd asked.

"I was supposed to meet Laura but Snake took my wheels," Brody said pathetically. "What with the cops'n all, I couldn't hang around. Laura thinks I didn't turn up."

He showed him Laura's message.

"Look at this."

Lloyd took a moment to read it.

"Yeah, you're in big trouble."

He shot a look at Laura sitting in a booth further back.

"And she is cute."

Brody turned and saw Laura laughing and joking with her friends. She clocked Brody and froze him with a chilly look. It was a heck of a performance. She knew what she was doing. You don't learn it; it's buried deep in those XX chromosomes.

Boys are defenceless.

Lloyd changed the subject.

"Did you get that power-out last night?"

Brody shrugged and waited for Lloyd to unload.

"Man, that screwed me big time. I was hacking the school servers. Those grades needed a little finessing. Didn't get out clean. Real messy."

Brody said, "Yeah, and I know what's doing it."

Lloyd ignored him and instead, offered his usual list of conspiracy theories.

"There weren't no storms, so what was it? Solar flares you think? Some kinda cyber-attack on our critical infrastructure?"

Lloyd's imagination could go to some strange places.

"I know, maybe the government's testing that secret anti-alien weapon I was telling you about. The one that sucks electricity out of the grid when they fire it up."

Brody laughed.

"Man, you've got some weird shit floating around in that noodle of yours, Lloyd."

"Yeah, weird - right up to the moment an alien raps on your door looking for a tasty meal of human brains. And gives you an eye-popping, two-million-volt shot in the tentacles," Lloyd insisted.

Brody laughed again as he shook his head.

"Look, if I tell you, you gotta keep it to yourself."

Lloyd said, "Yeah, sure," he mimes a zip across his lips. "Not a word."

"I'm serious, Lloyd. Really. Zip closed, yeah? It's important."

Lloyd got serious at last.

"Now I am curious, Brody boy. Sure, a state secret. They can cook me in oil, pull my teeth out and make me suck the boils on grandpa's hairy ass."

Steve arrived with the shakes.

"It's customary to tip your waiter, OK? Even jerks like you."

"Here's a tip." Lloyd gave him the finger.

Brody waited for Steve to leave.

"It's old Figgy," he said secretively.

"What's old Figgy?"

"The power cuts."

"Wait. It's Figgy that's responsible for the power outs? Come on Brody. Old Figgy? Think about it."

"That weird light the other night? It's a nuclear fusion reactor he's working on."

"And when did he tell you this?" Lloyd said doubtfully.

"I was at his house. He showed me how it works. But last night he cranked up the power."

"He invited you to his house? Don't you think that's creepy?"

"It's not like that," Brody said defensively. "Look, there're scientists around the world doing huge experiments and can't make it work, but he's got it running in his back bedroom. It's the power-up that's causing the power-out. I saw it for myself!" Lloyd was sceptical.

"And since when were you an expert on all that nuclear fusion bull, Brody boy?

"Don't call me that."

"Snake calls you that."

"Yeah, but I don't like it, OK?"

"If you say so, Mr. Brody Boyle. Boy genius and all-round clever dude. So, why are you so sure?"

"I think he knows what he's doing. He's invented something different, and well, I believe him."

As he sucked a sip from his shake, Brody spotted Snake and Baggy gliding past the café window, yelling like banshees.

"What the...?"

He got up and rushed out into the street just in time to see Snake and Baggy tearing down the sidewalk on electric scooters - scattering people like nine pins.

Lloyd stepped out into the street. They glanced at each other.

"Sick!" said Lloyd appreciatively.

Steve joined them with the check.

"What about my tip, losers?"

All three stared down the high street.

Brody had a question.

"What's he done with my wheels?"

20

"OK, Mom, I'm off now. You'll be OK?"

His mother's condition had eased a little. In a rare, lucid moment, she acknowledged Harry.

"I'll be fine. You worry too much."

Harry had his laptop with him as usual, stuffed in a plastic bag. He had locked his workshop door and was just checking in on his mother before he left for work.

"I'll be fine. You worry too much." His mom said, her voice a little brighter today.

Harry let Schrodinger slip into the room as he closed his mother's bedroom door, He paused for a moment.

Harry was a prisoner of his own obsessive condition. He opened the door again, to check that the cat was in fact in the room and in good health. It was.

That confirmed, he headed downstairs and out into the street where his old wreck of a car was parked.

***

The Plymouth Duster might have been a classic in better condition. But the paint fade, the rust, the fender dings and dents and the missing hub caps, they all took a chunk out of the resale value.

Then there was the suspension collapse, the threadbare carpets and the shabby seats covered in the parted seams of sun crisped vinyl. It wasn't much more than a junkyard on wheels.

He pushed the key in and twisted it. The five litre, V8 engine fired up after a couple of long wheezing turns of the starter motor and a coughing fit from the carburettor.

He pushed the stick into drive and motored off leaving behind a cloud of blue smoke and an oil stain where the old boat had been.

***

Watching from across the road the two spies kept the windows shut until the toxic smell had eased.

They'd been parked there since breakfast. It was now mid-morning.

They guessed that with such a late start, Harry Figg was probably a part-timer. Now at last, they could get down to the business they had been sent to do.

The doors to the SUV opened. Roberts and Torres stepped out and were instantly hit by the suffocating humidity. They snuck across the road to Harry's house, hacked through the undergrowth at the side of the property and past the rotting shed Brody had climbed a couple of nights ago. Like fearless explorer's discovering a hidden temple in a remote jungle, they finally made it to the back entrance.

Roberts used his arm to wipe the sweat from his face.

"Jeez, I'm already done with this place."

For once, Torres agreed, "Yeah, If the climate doesn't kill you the wild life will. Come on. Sooner we get this done, the sooner we get out of here."

The wooden panel door had warped with age and no longer fitted the frame as it used to decades ago. It didn't take much to slide the latch and gain access.

The door rubbed noisily against the jam before it swung open with a squeak on its old hinges. Inside it was dark and forbidding. They stood still and listened for a moment.

Nothing.

The old house permeated an unnerving stillness. Roberts shivered.

"This is where the audience shout, 'Don't go down to the cellar,'" he whispered.

Torres was a little more sanguine.

"Oh, I don't know. I love these old period properties. Just needs some TLC."

"Yeah, and a shed load of money."

Torres refocussed on the business at hand.

"Come on," she said. We've got work to do."

They checked the ground floor silently and professionally.

In the kitchen, Roberts found the cookie jar, cracked it open and took a couple.

Torres saw him stuff one into his mouth, crumbs spilling on the floor.

She gave him a look of distain that told him what she thought of his spook skills. With a tilt of her head she indicated he should follow as she crept upstairs.

She pointed at a door for Roberts to inspect while she went down the hall to check the rooms at the front.

Of the two bedrooms, only one had a bed. Other than that, they were just crammed with junk. But more interestingly, she saw lots of technical stuff and lab gear that someone like Figg would need for his experiments.

She went back down the hall to where Roberts was waiting.

Roberts whispered that he'd found a woman asleep, so they need to be extra quiet. Having said that, he threw the second cookie up to his mouth. It missed and fell with a soft tap onto the bare wooden floorboards.
Torres just shook her head in despair.

They crossed the few steps to the room opposite. It was Torres who managed to find the floorboard that moaned under her shoe. Roberts delighted in giving her the same scornful look she'd given him.
Behind them, Schrodinger was busy inspecting the cookie.

Roberts twisted the knob but the door was locked.
From inside his bomber jacket, he pulled out a lock pick wallet and removed a couple of slim instruments.
He inserted both into the lock at tangents to each other and worked them skilfully until, with a satisfying click, the door opened to Harry's workshop.
They stepped inside.

***

This, Torres thought, was interesting. She began examining what she took to be the fusion reactor. She snapped some photos while Roberts installed a camera on a shelf that faced the device.

As he worked, the bottom edge of his jacket caught a screwdriver lying on the work bench. It wasn't much but it moved very slightly.

He noticed Torres looking perplexed.

"What's up?" he whispered.

"It's much smaller than I was expecting."

"That's a good thing, yeah?" said Roberts.

"Maybe. There's no computer, and I can't find any written notes. There should be. That's where all the technical stuff would be."

"He had a shopping bag. Maybe he takes it all with him," Roberts wondered.

Torres said, "Well, that's just unfriendly."

"What do you want to do? Turn it on?"

Torres was horrified. "Christ no. That thing is dangerous. Let's..."

A voice from across the hallway interrupted her.

"Is that you Harry?"

"Damn!" Torres muttered.

They wait a few seconds. Nothing. Just silence. Torres pointed to the spherical core of the device.

"That's the interesting bit. We'll have to come back."

They slipped out of the workshop into the hall and were shocked to be confronted by a frail old lady in a night gown.

"Harry? You've brought your sister home."

Torres immediately guessed the old woman's condition. She'd seen the symptoms before when her father succumbed to a similar memory erasing disease. That was nearly eighteen months ago. It still hurt.

She helped the woman back to her bed.

"Harry and I are going to make you some coffee. You wait here." Torres said.

"I don't like coffee," Harry's mom complained. "You know I don't like coffee. It makes me nervous."

"Sure, tea it is. OK?" Torres assured her.

They left the room, closed the door and started down the stairs. Halfway down, Torres' shoe snagged on the torn carpet. She tripped, but Roberts caught her.

Recovering, she hissed: "Christ! This place is a goddamned health hazard!"

***

Back in the SUV, Roberts fiddled with his laptop, trying to get a picture from the hidden camera. The image was frustratingly intermittent.

"This cheap software. You'd think The Corporation could afford top of the range."

Suddenly the picture snapped on. A solid image. Roberts was relieved. He still blanched from the cookie incident.

"OK. It's cool. We have eyes on." He bragged. His voice suddenly full of authority and competence.

"How about you. What did you make of it?"

Torres was browsing through the pictures she'd taken.

"These aren't going to satisfy the people back at head office. It looks like a pile of junk. God knows how it works."

The hidden camera view of the 'pile of junk' in Harry's workshop that Roberts was looking at, wasn't 4K, but it was clear enough.

"It just looks so amateurish," he said.

He counted on his fingers. "Albert Einstein, Robert Oppenheimer, Stephen Hawking, and now, Harry Figg? Are you sure it's all the eggheads back at the Corporation think it is, and not just a pile of scrap?"

"No, Figg is definitely on to something," Torres said confidently. "He's come at it out of left field. I don't know how. His mind just works differently."

Roberts shut the software down and closed the laptop.

"Whatever. So far, The Corporation's spent a shed load of bucks for very little bang."

"Yes, well, Harry Figg's fusion experiment just might save their corporate asses." Torres said.

She put the car into gear and they drove off.

21

It was afternoon at the school gates. Students were either heading home or just hanging around with their friends. Brody was loitering miserably hoping to see Laura.

He spotted her with some friends who helpfully, pointed him out. She looked over and gave him a stare that would freeze hell.

He mustered the courage to go over. He didn't get far. Baggy headed him off on his new electric scooter.

"What's up, Brody. You seen Lloyd?"

Brody kept a watchful eye on Laura as he replied.

"Well, he was in school. You tried his cell?"

"Yeah, nothing," Baggy said. "What do you think of the scooter, pretty smooth eh?"

"Yeah, very cool. Must be expensive," Brody said.

"Na, Snake's got contacts. Big discount. He'll cut you a deal, but you gotta be quick. Hotcakes man."

Brody ignored him and went straight to the question that had been bugging him.

"Where's my bike, Baggy?"

This stopped Baggy's pitch dead in its tracks. "What? Your bike?

"Yeah. You and Snake took it the other night." Brody said.

"Yeah, well. What, you don't want one of these?"

"Where am I going to get that kind of money. I just want my wheels," Brody insisted.

"You don't even know how much yet." Baggy was still pitching.

"My bike. Come on Benedict. I need it." He rarely used Baggy's given name. This was serious.

As Baggy rode away. "Be at the lot tonight. OK?"

He motored over to try his luck with another group of kids.

In the time between Baggy's sales pitch and Brody's question, Laura had left with her friends. He pulled out his cell and sent a message. He was determined to fix things between them.

"Laura, pls meet me at the Jake O 2night. I can xplain."

22

Later, in the science prep room where Harry worked, a knock on the door was ignored. And, as usual, Penny Wallace entered anyway.

"I've got some visitors for you, Harry."

Harry's eyes were glued to the data on his laptop screen.

"Sorry? Visitors? For me? No. I'm too busy. I don't have time." Harry insisted.

"They say it's important." Penny was always polite despite Harry's prickliness, but her patience was wearing thin.

"Perhaps just this once? Just as a courtesy, Harry?"

She turned to whoever was in the room behind her and showed them in.

"This is Mr. Figg," she said as she looked at her watch. "Be quick. I've got a home life."

Harry looked up from the screen, irritated at the interruption, and waited.

"Mr Harry Figg? I'm Torres. This is Roberts."

Harry was not happy with the intrusion. With any interruption really. His social skills were, to say the least, shaky. He slammed the laptop closed and slid it into the plastic shopping bag along with his notes.

"I'm very busy. This is very inconvenient." He looked at his watch and stood up. "Yes, I really should be going."

"Please, give us a moment Mr. Figg," Roberts said firmly.

Torres was more direct.

"I'll come straight to the point. Your research has come to the attention of my client,' she said. "I'll be honest with you Mr. Figg, they're quite giddy with excitement - and for good reason."

"I keep my work to myself. Nothing is published. How could you, or whoever your client is, know anything about my research?"

Roberts throws a name in, "Well, that's not quite true is it. - Edward Schtole at MIT?"

"We have communicated. He's been very encouraging," Harry revealed.

He became more agitated and started gathering his things. "It's a private matter. Perhaps you'd better leave."

Torres took her laptop from her briefcase, opened it to a series of emails and showed them to Harry.

"Those are my emails to Eddy. How..?"

Torres played her card, "Edward Schtole is in fact Ron Cable, a senior partner at my clients' company. You've been telling your secrets to him for the last few months."

Harry's legs weakened with the shock of the revelation. He collapsed back into the chair and stared up at the two intruders.

"Not Eddy? Isn't that fraud or something?" Then a smug smile crossed his face, "I guess they didn't get very far did they."

Torres countered, "That's the problem and I'm here to fix it. The Corporation has instructed me to make you an offer."

Roberts butted in, "Think very carefully before you answer Mr. Figg."

"How do you even know I have a working prototype?"

"The power outs are a big calling card," Torres said. "And the x-rays and other particle emissions? There's no doubt about it, Mr Figg - you've got a star in a jar."

She looked at the curious and baffling old man staring up at her. He deserved more credit she decided.

"No. More than that. You've built a stable fusion reactor and The Corporation wants to know how you did it."

Harry relaxed back in his chair, "No, I have no interest in your money so screw The Corporation and you can leave now."

"Mrs. Wallace! PENNY!" he shouted.

The temperature dropped to frosty.

Torres tried persuasion, "Don't be so hasty, Mr. Figg. We could give you all the lab equipment you need to finish your work."

Penny stepped into the room and sensed the tension.

"Everything OK, Harry?"

"These people are just leaving." Harry said emphatically.

She stepped back to let them pass.

"I'm sorry you feel that way," said Roberts. The threat in his voice undisguised.

As she gathered her own laptop, Torres announced flatly, "I hope you don't come to regret that decision, Mr. Figg." She snapped a business card onto the desk, "Think about it."

They both paused for a moment to give Harry a cold, hard stare. Then turned and left.

Penny said, "What was that all about Harry?"

Harry was thoughtful.

"For the first time in my life someone doesn't think I'm an irrelevant joke."

23

Some days are worse than others.

Brody arrived home from school to find the front door kicked open and the wooden door-jam splintered. He stepped over the threshold into the hall and paused to listen. He held his breath but the house remained silent.

The door to the living room was shut. He crept quietly over to it, turned the handle, nervously eased the door open and entered.

The room was empty.

He stepped back out into the hallway and paused, listening again for any movement.

From behind, a hand reached silently to smother his mouth. Shocked, Brody turned and found his mother standing there, eyes wide with terror. She pulled him into the kitchen, put her finger to her lips and closed the door.

She had a nasty red welt on her cheek and a drip of blood hanging from her nose.

"Clayton," she whispered. "He's upstairs. Came back drunk. I think he's asleep in the bedroom."

Brody couldn't hide his alarm, "What's he doing here Mom, I thought you said he wasn't coming back."

"I didn't let him in," said Rachel. "I've called the police. Let's just keep quiet until they get here, yes?"

Brody pulled away from his mother and stepped back out into the hall.

"I've got to get something, Mom."

"You can't go up there, Brody." There was fear in her voice.

"It's important. It'll be OK."

He was already on the stairs. She tugged on his arm, "No, Brody!" she whispered hoarsely.

His mother watched horrified as Brody crept up. He could see into his mother's bedroom through the banister spindles. Clayton was lying restlessly on the bed.

Brody continued up to the landing, tiptoed into his bedroom and took the press cutting pinned to the wall. He folded it into his pocket and...

"You! 'Bout time I put you out of my misery, boy."

Brody turned and was shocked to see the swaying figure of Clayton in the doorway. He was already removing his belt, ready to administer the correction he believed the boy was due.

Then a scream as Rachel came up from behind and charged him like a quarterback, throwing Clayton to the floor. Only the blind rage of a mother protecting her child could have given her such fearless strength.

Brody couldn't believe what he was seeing. His mother sat astride Clayton, shouting, beating, scratching and kicking as she vent her rage on the bully.

She shouted for Brody to get out – now!

But her young son was transfixed, astonished at his mother's fury.

Then, from downstairs, a voice.

"Mrs Boyle? Rachel?" Deputy Fiennes shouted.

Brody rushed down.

"Quick! Mom. She's up there."

Dave Fiennes didn't hesitate. He rushed upstairs with the new recruit, towards the screaming and shouting.

It didn't take long to subdue Rachel's ex. Brody watched as the younger officer brought the drunk down, handcuffed and still struggling. Bloody scratches across Clayton's face told of the pent-up anger his mother had unleashed on him.

A few minutes later, Fiennes gently helped the tearful Rachel downstairs. It was clear they had a connection and Dave Fiennes was smitten.

"This time you've got to press assault charges, Rachel," Dave appealed to her. "That son of a bitch is dangerous."

"I don't know, Dave. When he's drunk no restraining order will stop him," she said.

Dave turned to Brody, "I'm taking your mom to the station. We're just going to take a statement, that's all. You got any friends or neighbours you can stay with for an hour or two?"

Brody gave his mom a reassuring look, "Don't worry Mom. I'm going to meet Laura."

"Laura?"

Laura was news to Rachel.

24

Early evening and things were slow at the Jake O. At the register, the sports pages rustled as they were turned. Jake seemed to have no home life.

He called over to the evening help to bring him tea. Steve was still there putting in the hours for pocket cash. Maybe he had no home life to speak of either.

***

Laura was sitting in a booth. Her two friends, Beth and Stacey were sitting opposite. The conversation was about Brody and Laura was listening.

Beth was saying, "Definitely not!"

Laura wondered what Stacey thought.

"I don't know. Maybe you should hear him out?"

"You're such a wimp Stacey," Beth said. "You don't give boys like that a second chance."

"Boys like what, Beth?" Laura found herself defending Brody.

"You know. His family, his friends. They're trouble," Beth declared.

Stacey took a different view. "Maybe, but he is cute." She caught a look from Laura and added. "...in a rough sort of way."

Laura did the math.

"OK. One for. One against," she said. "I'm not sure affairs of the heart have anything to do with democracy but you're right Beth. He could be trouble but there's more to him. He's actually really clever and thoughtful and yes, maybe his family don't have much but how does that make him a bad person?

I don't know why he didn't make it the other day, so, like you say, Stacey, maybe I should give him a chance to explain? And he is kinda cute'n all..."

She was interrupted when waiter Steve arrived and sidled in right next to Laura.

"Hi ladies. What's up?"

Then to Laura, "Did you miss me hot lips? You girls need a guy like me to show you a good time."

Beth almost threw up. Laura slid further back into the booth, away from Steve. Not that he'd recognise a 'not-interested' signal if it was branded on his forehead with a hot iron.

Stacey said, "Hey, Steve. Laura was stood up. D'ya think she should give the guy another chance?"

He didn't get a chance to answer. Jake shouted across from the register.

"What, are you a customer today? Not on wages? Great! I can make a profit at last."

Steve shouted back, "Yeah, gimme a moment." He turned back to the girls, "What is it with the Irish."

"Irish?" Laura queried.

"Yeah, the boss, Jake O'Bean."

The three girls burst out laughing.

Laura explained between giggles.

"Well, Jake's not Irish. And the place isn't called 'Jake O'Bean'," she said it with an Irish accent. "It's a play on Jacobean. You know? - the British Jacobean period? Jamestown? Virginia?"

Beth added, "Jake O Bean – like, coffee bean?"

"Yeah, of course. I knew that. I was, you know, kidding." Steve tried to cover his embarrassment.

From the cash register, "Customers!"

"Coming Jake," said Steve. "Be back girls. Don't go without me."

They watched him leave and started sniggering.

"Well, that decides it." Laura declared.

Beth and Stacey, "What does?"

"I'm giving Brody another chance."

25

The routine in the Figg household was as regular as an atomic clock. Harry in the kitchen making hot chocolate for his mother, same time each evening. The Persian cat mooching up and down the kitchen counter as he worked.

He set the mug and a plate of cookies on the tray and paused, hovering expectantly for the inevitable call from his mother.

"Harry?"

There it was.

"Coming Mom."

It was the same every day since her condition got worse.

On the counter was an unopened envelope. He placed that on the tray as well. Schrodinger jumped down, scrambled around Harry and led the way up-stairs.

He entered his mother's room and went through the usual. "Here's your hot chocolate," followed by the "I don't like hot chocolate," routine.

"Yes, you do Mom, you always have hot chocolate," he said, with more than a little tired resignation in his voice.

"Your sister was here this afternoon. She made me tea."

"No, she didn't Mom. Now sit up. Let's put your talking book on."

Her son's denial of what for her was a simple truth, angered her.

"She was here with you. Don't you remember? You were in your work room - like you always are. You and your silly hobby. You never have time for me."

There was a long pause before Harry replied.

"This afternoon? Two people? My sister and someone else?"

Harry dashed out of the room and across the hall to his workshop. He used his key but was surprised to find the door unlocked.

His mother called from her bed, "She was going to make me coffee. She knows I don't like coffee."

He entered, dropped the envelope on the work bench and looked around carefully.

***

Outside, in the SUV, the spies were watching Harry on Roberts' laptop. They could see him scanning the room.

His head swivelled from one end of the room to the other, up and down and along the work bench until his eyes fixed on a screwdriver. He turned it slightly until it was perfectly aligned with the row of other tools.

Torres understood. "He knows."

"I swear, I didn't touch anything." Roberts said defensively.

26

The sun had set an hour or so ago. Brody hadn't noticed. He sat forlornly in the front of the van on what would have been a seat, if the stuff that usually covered the metal frame hadn't been ripped out years ago.

He'd been there for a while, as gloomy as the evening light. The noise of wheels crunching on the gravel made him look up.

"Hi Lloyd. You got one too – nice," Brody said with little interest.

Lloyd leant the scooter against a rusty panel of the van.

"Oh yeah, it's insane. How about you?"

Brody said, "Me? You know that's not going to happen."

Somewhere, in the distance, came the sound of gunfire.

"You still hanging around with old Figgy?" Lloyd asked.

"Yeah, well, you know - he's OK."

"How about Laura. You fixed that?"

"I dunno. Maybe."

The sound of small arms was getting closer. They both looked up as Snake and Baggy flew around the corner on their e-scooters, randomly throwing firecrackers and yelling like rodeo riders.

They skidded to a dirt-spraying halt right next to Brody and Lloyd.

"Subtle," Lloyd said. Brody liked Lloyd's quiet humour.

Flashing bundles of cash, Snake said, "Been a good day, and my guy can get more. I'll give you cash on every sale you make. What'd you say."

Lieutenant Baggy pitched in, "How about it, fellas? Wanna make some easy bucks?"

"Yeah, I could use some cash," Lloyd said.

"Right now, all I want are my wheels, Snake."

"That's old news Brody boy," said Snake. "This is the future. All the kids'll be riding 'em. Here, jump on. - Take it for a spin."

"I don't have time, Snake. I need my bike?"

"Come on Snake, he needs his wheels. Stop being an asshole," Lloyd said. "It's over there, behind the office."

The office was a converted and long abandoned container, from the days when the lot was earmarked for housing.

Brody set off to retrieve his wheels, but the "whoop" of a police siren made him duck out of sight.

Spying from behind a pile of debris he watched as a police cruiser pulled up in a hurry, bar lights blinking. Two cops got out and strafed the lot with flashlights.

Through the open window of the saloon, Officer Fiennes shouted a warning,

"Stay where you are!"

He stepped out and from the kerbside, lit up the trio with his flashlight.

"You kids been throwing fireworks?"

He spotted Snake. "You! McKay! I want to talk to you. You been boosting booze again?"

Snake, Baggy and Lloyd didn't hang around to answer questions. They grabbed their scooters and raced off in three different directions.

Fiennes made a final sweep with the flashlight and got back in the car.

The beam had skimmed the top of Brody's head. He was sure Dave had seen him, but the cop car revved its motor and sped off, wheels spinning, so he guessed not.

The bike was where Lloyd said it was. Brody climbed on and peddled off like an Olympian circuit racer. He was desperate to see Laura. He was already late.

Screwing up was not an option.

27

"Face it, Laura, he's not coming," Beth said.

Beth and Stacey were getting restless to leave the Jake O. Conversation had come to a standstill.

Stacey tried to be supportive, "You gave him a chance. He's a fool."

"Plenty of fish," said Beth.

"Tastier ones," quipped Stacey.

Beth agreed, "Yeah, he's such a jerk.

Laura was thoughtful, "I guess you're right. I'm just wasting my time."

There was a brief hiatus, as though with those final words, the matter was settled. Then Beth and Stacey got up to leave.

"You coming Laura?" Stacey asked as she paid her check.

"Yeah - be along," she hesitated, but then followed as far as the cash register. She put the check on the counter and left some cash.

"Give Steve the change, Jake."

With the wisdom of age, Jake gave Laura some good advice. "Your money's wasted on him Laura."

Then her phone buzzed. It was a message from Brody.

"Sorry, nearly there x."

"Yeah. I'm a mug for lost causes," Laura told Jake. They both laughed. But Jake was already checking the scores on the sports pages.

***

Out on the street, sparks flew from Brody's wheels as he raced to keep his promise.

He threw the bike to the ground outside the Jake O and rushed in, eagerly scanning the room.

It was mostly empty tables and booths and no sign of Laura.

He couldn't hide his disappointment.

"Hey Jake. You seen Laura?"

Jake didn't look up from the pages, "Well, she was here a while ago."

Then came a familiar voice from behind that made his heart beat faster.

"So, Brody Boyle, what's your story?"

***

In a booth at the back of the Jake O, Brody and Laura were sipping sodas. She had just read the press cutting.

"You're saying old Figgy's got one of these at home?"

"Yeah, It's a scientific breakthrough." Brody said.

"Says you. Why did you think I wanted to see it?"

Brody considered that for a moment.

"Well, Laura, I'm not - you know - I haven't got much." Brody struggled to put his thoughts into words. "But I thought, well, if I could just show you this, star in a jar - that would be something wouldn't it?"

"You can't put a star in a jar, Brody," Laura declared with simple logic.

"No, but you can create the fusion that burns inside every star - if you know how. It's not an easy thing to do."

"And you're telling me that's what old Figgy's done? Our old Figgy. The lab guy at school?"

"Aren't you curious?" Brody teased.

Laura thought about that for a moment. Then came the words that made the star in Brody's young heart burn brighter.

"I don't care what you have, Brody. Money and such. Some boys make all kinds of promises. They tell girls foolish things, like how they'll climb mountains for you, or buy you diamonds, or give you the moon'n all."

Laura had consumed a lot of romantic novels.

"But you want to take me to a star. That's very romantic, Brody. How could a girl refuse?"

28

"Who's the girl?" Harry said when he opened the door and saw Brody and Laura standing there. "Why don't you bring the whole school? Invite the whole town?"

"It's just Laura," Brody explained. "She's interested. I thought you wouldn't mind, Mr Figg."

"Hello Mr Figg," Laura said demurely.

Harry did a quick check up and down the street.

"I think The Corporation's trying to steal the fusion reactor," he muttered furtively.

He turned and headed back up the stairs.

"Close the door behind you."

Brody followed behind Laura.

"Mind the carpet, Laura, it's a death trap."

***

In Harry's workshop the reactor was in pieces.

He took a component from a box and started fixing it into place.

"Oh, it's broken?" Brody wondered. He was keen for Laura to see it working. To keep his promise.

"I've made some improvements to the confinement chamber. The inside is coated with a special material that reduces emissions."

"Why, was it dangerous before?" asked Brody.

"Not for the short experimental runs that I've been doing. Now it's more stable it can run for considerably longer," he said. "It's best to be safe."

Luara crouched down to stroke Schrodinger. She looked up, "So I won't be able to see the star, Mr Figg?"

"Soon as I've fixed these parts."

While Harry continued reassembling the reactor, Brody spotted the envelope, still unopened, on the work bench. He turned it to read the postmark.

"It's from Cambridge – Massachusetts. Aren't you gonna read it? Looks important."

Harry picked it up, weighed it in his hand. Then discarded it casually."

"Maybe. When I find time."

A thought suddenly hit Brody.

"Whoa, wait a minute. You said you think someone's trying to steal the reactor?"

"They offered me money, Brody. I turned them down. They've already sent people to break into my lab! It's The Corporation. They want my invention and they'll do anything to get it."

"Maybe I can help?" Brody suggested.
"What can a kid like you do Brody?"
"You'd be surprised, Mr Figg. I've got friends."

***

Outside, parked up in the SUV, the spies were watching Harry on the laptop. Torres was on her cell phone to The Corporation."

"I told you, he's not interested in money."

While she listened to the reply, she gave Roberts a snide shake of her head to show her contempt for her client.

"Yes, I'm aware we need to get this done asap. Figg's working on it right now. We'll have to try later. I'll get back to you."

***

"OK, that should do it," Harry said as he tightened a cable connector. "This should really zap the power up."

Then with less confidence, "Oh, you two better stand back - just in case."

The two high school kids took a few steps back.

He pulled a power lever and a low hum filled the room. Other equipment was switched on in sequence: meters, gauges and display screens came alive. Schrodinger scrambled out of the room when the pump started up and began its noisy pounding.

Harry muttered to himself while he checked readouts and made notes.

"Inertial Electrostatic Confinement on standby. Deuterium levels active. Vacuum increasing. Voltage approaching capacity limits. Fusion initiator - stable."

Laura looked nervously at Brody. She took his hand. He gave hers a squeeze. If his heart was a fusion reactor, it would be glowing already.

Harry nudged the power control up slowly. As he did, the violet light flickered on and started radiating through the glass porthole. It continued to grow brighter as the droning sound increased.

If he hadn't heard it before he might have found the noise unnerving. Laura gave Brody more anxious looks. He squeezed her hand again to reassure her.

That's when the neighborhood power flickered out again.

***

In the SUV, the laptop screen glowed brightly, bathing the occupants in an eerie violet light. Torres reached for her detector and scanned for emissions. Not a sound came from it. She turned a control and whacked it a couple of times, but still nothing.

She gave Roberts a shrug of surprise.

"That's weird," she said.

***

Harry was doing the very same test, waving an emission detector over the reactor.

"Good, the coating works. Like a bullet proof vest, all the x-rays and gamma rays stay inside the fusion chamber."

Brody and Laura were still standing at the far end of the room by the window. Laura looked at Brody expectantly.

"So, Mr. Figg..." Brody said.

"Call me Harry, Brody."

"OK - Harry - is it safe for Laura to take a look?"

Harry assured him it was.

The light seemed to fill the room as Laura nervously took the few steps towards the strange machine. Her eyes were full of wonder as the light from the 'star' flickered across her face.

"You're right Brody. It is a star."

Brody looked on proudly.

"Every star should have a name, isn't that so, Harry"

Even a socially awkward soul like Harry could see Brody's infatuation with the girl.

"I guess we could choose any name we like," he said. "Why don't we call this one 'Laura'?"

29

"What's up Lloyd?" Brody said over the muted buzz of excitement in the school corridor. Baggy was spreading the word to a group of students nearby.

"You haven't heard? It's a scooter race. Snake's fixed it. After school. Thursday."

Brody pointed to a poster pinned to a bulletin board.

"That's the night of the Science Fair. What's in it for Snake?"

Baggy butted in. "What do you think, Brodeo? We're taking bets on the winner."

"I guess that'll be Snake?" Brody said cynically.

"The Crew," Baggy said. "We all get a share."

"Shame you don't have one," said Lloyd. "You'll make some easy money."

Brody shrugged, "Isn't the schoolyard going to be busy at that time?"

Baggy didn't think so.

"No problemo. We wait till everyone's inside the hall with their kid's stupid cardboard science junk.

"Where to?" Brody asked.

"Where do you think? Snake Crew corner lot. Jungle rules - any way you can."

Penny Wallace arrived and she smelt trouble.

"What's going on Lloyd Ferris? Benedict Marchant?"

She looked up and down the corridor at the other groups of students.

"You kids are up to something."

"Us, miss? No, we're cool," Baggy assured her.

Lloyd was already slipping away, "I'm late, Miss. I don't need another tardy."

Then Baggy slinked away and caught up with Lloyd, leaving Ms Wallace with Brody.

"How about you, Brody?"

He shrugged again.

"Your science grades have been pretty good recently. You're really taking an interest."

She thumbed at the Science Fair poster behind her. "You going to enter? I think you should. Time's running out."

"I don't have a project. Maybe I'll think about it."

What Brody was mostly thinking about these days was Laura.

"Make it a crowd pleaser. It'll push your grades up." Penny said.

And as she started to walk away.

"You've got talent, Brody. Don't waste it."

Brody watched her leave. Her words had given him an idea.

"A crowd pleaser? Hmmm," he said thoughtfully, just as Harry Figg ambled past on his way to the science classroom.

"Hey, Mr. Figg - er - Harry."

Harry stopped, turned and waited.

"You got a moment, Harry?"

***

The SUV drove slowly down Harry's avenue. It was deserted except for an older man walking his dog. "Car's gone - looks like he's not there," Roberts said.

Roberts and Torres were eyeballing Harry's house, looking for an opportunity to break in and snatch the device. They both knew they had to up their game.

Torres pointed to the blank laptop screen, "Well, if you'd have charged the batteries in the camera we'd know for sure, wouldn't we," she said. "Listen, you're in as a favour. No more screw-ups! Let's get this done."

***

Brody was standing in the doorway to the science lab annex. Harry was in his chair, his face a picture of astonishment. He couldn't believe what he'd just heard.

"You want to what?"

"For the Science Fair," Brody said. "We can set it up between us. Miss Wallace says I need something impressive – to improve my grades."

"What about the water electrolysis experiment?"

"Yeah, well, it's not exactly a crowd pleaser, is it."

"No, but at least it would be your work. Isn't the fusion reactor a tad above ninth grade?"

Brody wouldn't be put off.

"Of course. It's your thing, but you can give me the skinny on how it works - you know - I can talk about that?"

"You want a crash course in Quantum Mechanics?" Harry was speechless.

Brody just shrugged naively.

"By Thursday!"

30

A little further up the avenue an e-scooter had been keeping pace with the SUV.

When Torres parked up, the scooter stopped and a cowboy boot stepped onto the road.

Snake watched as the two industrial spies got out and entered the grounds of Harry's property.

He waited just a little longer, then set off after them, making sure to keep out of sight. He knew how to do it – he'd watched all the spy shows and crime dramas on TV.

They had gained entranced to Harry's house in the same way they had before. But this time, they knew to look out for the old lady. So, no noise and no cookies!

Outside, in the 'jungle', Snake had reached the back door. He was thinking that, maybe, in an act of self-preservation and despite his natural ability and unique skill set, he should arm himself with a weapon of some sort. Those spy guys just might have skill sets of their own.

He retraced his steps back to the shed and forced his way in through the rotting door. It had jammed open just a crack and it took some shoving to open it enough for him to slide through.

Standing amongst the junk strewn floor he found exactly what he needed.

***

Roberts was reading the press cuttings on the wall of Harry's workshop. There was one that mentioned the Corporation. Its headline: 'Corporation Fusion Claim Rejected'.

"Hey, the Corporation's getting some stinking PR. You know about this?"

"Roberts!" Torres exclaimed in frustration, her voice a stage whisper. "Jesus! Just disconnect everything that goes to the core. That's the bit we want."

"It's not dangerous? Radioactive?"

"Only when it's on, idiot. Grab some tools."

***

A tattooed hand slid stealthily up the handrail leading to the second-floor landing. Treading gently, Snake took each stair slowly. At eye level to the floor, peering through the banister spindles, he could see an open door to a room across the hall.

Out of a shadowy corner came a flash of white fur as Schrodinger scampered across to the workshop.

Snake climbed the last few steps and snuck over. He stood for a moment in the doorway, spying on the spies.

The two Corporation agents were too busy to notice the intruder watching them. As he unplugged cables and connectors, Roberts said.

"Did you know the Corporation's on its financial ass?"

"Why do you think we're here? Word is the company's insolvent. Investors are worrying about getting their money back. This discovery could change everything."

The loud thud of iron on wood and an angry voice from the doorway launched Schrodinger into the arms of Torres. She turned with the cat still clinging to her, scratching and hissing.

"What are you assholes doing in old Figgy's crib?" Snake yelled.

The spies where shocked to see a tattooed youth standing there. He was smacking the door frame with a rusty iron pipe and looked ready to do some damage.

"Out!" Snake shouted.

He banged the pipe hard and noisy against the door frame again.

"NOW!"

"OK, kid - we don't want any trouble." Roberts said.

Torres was trying to divest herself of the terrified feline whose claws clung to her like burr grass. She shot Roberts a scornful glare.

Then things got complicated.

Unseen by Snake, the bedroom door had opened and out stepped the ghostly figure of Harry's mother.

"Harry? Where's my Harry?"

The cat leapt from Torres and ran over to hide behind Harry's mom. He peered out from behind her legs all haughty and resentful.

Snake turned and saw the old woman. This was unexpected.

The two spies didn't hang around. They slid past Snake and squeezed around Harry's mom to get to the stairs. Schrodinger got mixed up in their legs as he to, bolted for the stairs.

Shocked, Snake dropped the pipe and followed them.

Now, more confused than ever, Mrs. Figg appealed to the strangers, "What have you done with my Harry?"

Snake said, "Nothing. He ain't here. Sorry, lady. I'm just…"

He was just two steps down when his foot got caught in a torn patch of carpet.

"Oh shiiit!"

He stumbled forward and crashed into Torres, who crashed into Roberts.

The three of them – and Schrodinger - became a noisy, painful, head-over-heals avalanche that ended up in an undignified heap of bodies and cat fur at the bottom of the stairs.

31

"That's it! No more favors."

Brody and Laura were in a booth at the Jake O, when an angry and bruised Snake limped in and stood in the aisle next to them. He was truly unhappy.

"Yeah, but Harry says to say thanks. He really appreciates what you did."

This didn't placate the Snake Crew boss.

"He should be glad I don't sue his ass. Those stairs are lethal."

"I didn't know who else to ask, and, you know - we're the Snake Crew aren't we, 'all for one', like those three French guys?"

Snake peered at Brody through half closed eyes, trying to figure if he was being mocked.

"Yeah, well - next time, call the French guys."

He turned and hobbled away. Brody leant out and watched him leave the coffee house just as Lloyd and Baggy arrived.

Snake collared Baggy, "You! Come with me."

Lloyd wandered down and joined Brody and Laura.

"What's with Snake. He been hit by a bus?" Lloyd wondered.

"Harry's in trouble. Someone's trying to steal his fusion reactor," Brody explained.

Lloyd screwed his face and shrugged, "What's that got to do with Snake?"

Brody gave him the highlights. Lloyd was astonished to hear that Snake agreed to help the old man.

"Snake, trying to help old Figgy? Go figure," Lloyd said. "There's a warm and fuzzy side to him after all."

"Not today there isn't," Brody said.

"But who would do that, Brody?" Laura asked.

It took Brody a few seconds to catch up, then the penny dropped.

"The Corporation."

"What corporation?" Laura pressed.

"I don't know, some big outfit somewhere. They want to steal Harry's invention," Brody said.

Lloyd threw in his two cents, "If people want to steal it, it must be valuable," he said. "Who'd have thought. Old Figgy, on the Mission Impossible hit list right here in this lousy dump."

"Do you think he's in danger?" Laura wondered.

"If those two spies are the real deal, then he doesn't stand a chance." Brody said.

Lloyd's over-active imagination ramped it all up. "Yeah, they're probably highly trained professionals. Like you seen in those movies? Armed and extremely dangerous. Probably ex-Special Forces. The guys you call on when the aliens come to suck your brains out," he speculated wildly.

That image hung in the air for a moment. Then Brody piped up.

"Anyhow, I've got to go - you coming, Laura?"

"Where're we going?"

"Harry Figg's place - I gotta catch up on some science."

32

The weather had turned again. After a couple of mostly sunny days, hot winds blowing thunderheads up from the south were threatening rain – maybe something worse.

They were overdue a big storm. Jorden County was close enough to Tornado Alley to catch one every now and then.

What was certain though, the late summer humidity was stifling and making everyone cranky.

Torres was at the wheel as they drove through the city, jazz playing on the radio and the two of them bickering as usual.

Roberts had a black eye and his arm was strapped across his chest as a result of the tumble on Harry's stairs. He was griping about them being bested by a kid.

Torres didn't agree.

"Back it up, Roberts. That's why you're here. Protection. A kid and an old woman show up and you're the first out the door," she said. "Remind me - which Secret Service training manual did that strategy come from?"

Roberts said, "I didn't see you pull any Kung Fu shit."

Torres had to swerve to avoid a kid on a scooter. The rider gave her the one finger salute and a petulant look.

"So far, we haven't covered ourselves in glory. The Corporation needs results and you're going to have to start pulling your weight," she said.

"I work better on my own," Roberts claimed. "This assignment has been jinxed from the start. You had no plan."

Torres reaction was to turn the jazz up loud. She knew Roberts hated it. But it was some mellow John Coltrane sax that was playing which didn't get under Roberts' skin as much as she would have liked.

Some wild, off-key, Miles Davis trumpet would have done the job better. Fingernails scratching down a chalk board was how he heard it.

She raised her voice.

"No plan?! The plan was fine until you came on board. The Corporation forced me to take you along. What are you, the chairman's nephew?"

Roberts bridled, "I'm a highly experienced undercover operative. You just can't stand me second guessing your amateur plays. I'm ex CIA."

"Yeah, I saw you there, working reception. Give me a break!"

***

They drove in silence, apart for the music, until a few minutes later when they pulled up outside the school gates.

"What are we doing here?" Roberts queried miserably.

Torres turn the music down.

"Did you notice the posters last time we were here?" she said.

They got out and Torres strode over to a nearby school bulletin board near the gates.

"Take a look at this," she said.

Roberts joined her. A poster for the Science Fair was prominently displayed amongst the school announcements, community notices and messages.

Roberts didn't get it.

"It's a Science Fair. So what?"

"Figg knows we're on to him. He may be smart enough to hide the device in plain sight. This could be our opportunity."

Roberts was shocked, "Wait a minute, you think he's crazy enough to fire that thing up right here – in broad daylight?"

"Actually, it will be in the evening, after school hours."

Torres' cell buzzed. It was a number that required privacy. She moved away from the notice board and her associate and tapped the green button. Sneaking a look at Roberts, she turned her back and spoke in a hushed voice.

"Are you crazy? I said I'd call you…"

A pause as she listened. Then…

"Don't threaten me."

She stole another quick look at Roberts, then turned her back again.

"I'm working on something. I'll call you."

The call ended and she strolled back to the gates.

Roberts couldn't hide his curiosity – nor his suspicions.

"Something I should know about?"

"Private stuff. None of your beeswax."

The first heavy splat of warm rain hit the sidewalk.

33

On the night of the Science Fair at Jorden County High, the weather just felt heavy and ready to spill. Like a huge sponge that just couldn't hold any more moisture.

It had threatened ominously all day, but they seemed to have dodged a bullet. The news reported towns to the west getting hit pretty heavily by the late summer storms.

Overhead, the cloud cover only revealed itself when sheets of lightning jumped from one thunderhead to another in skittish leaps of shimmering incandescence, followed by a low, unhappy rumble of thunder.

***

In the sports gymnasium, science projects were being set up by excited students on long tables against three walls and in rows down the centre.

Groups of proud parents were hovering anxiously over their child's exhibit. Each student seemed to be struggling to coax their project into animated cardboard and paper mâché life, often accompanied by fizzes and bangs.

Others attempted more complex projects.

One smug student was boastfully displaying a working model of a hydroelectric dam, while her pushy parents observed the competition with haughty distain.

Like the one on the next table down. Brody and Laura were helping Harry assemble the reactor. A thick cable ran from the device and out through a nearby exit into an adjacent service room. A sign on the door warned: 'Mains Supply – DANGER'.

***

A buzz spread around the gym as the school principal, escorted by assorted flunkies, inspected each project.

Principal Jarvis was tall, balding and so whippet skinny he looked like a sudden gust would blow him over. But counter intuitively, the principal was a man entirely lacking in principles.

He reached the student with the hydroelectric dam exhibit and didn't hide his enthusiasm.

"Very good. Excellent work, Jody." He gave a knowing wink to her parents.

The student gloated with smug entitlement. Her parents bristled with pride and sniffed dismissively at the mess on the next table along.

Jarvis seemed to share the hydroelectric family's opinion.

He and his entourage glided over to Brody and Harry's table. A local photographer snapped pictures as the group of dignitaries shook their heads dismissively and joked about the unfinished display.

The principal had an eye on a political career when his tenure at Jordon County High was done. That's why he had invited a number of city administrators to take part in the judging. He'd enticed them with the promise of a picture and a name check in the local press.

Jarvis didn't hide his distain.
"Well, this is all a bit of a mess. Is it ever going to work - whatever it is?"
There were smirks and sniggers from the hydroelectric family watching a table away.
Brody tried to be positive.
"Well, I think so..."
Harry was more forthright, "Oh, yes. We're just making the final adjustments."

Jarvis glanced across to the hydroelectric family and shook his head disparagingly. A shared joke. He moved on to the next exhibit.

Young Brody couldn't see how he stood a chance.

But before the judging even got underway, it was the concern on the inventor's face that really worried him.

"What's up Harry. Everything OK?"

"It was a bit unstable last time I turned it on. When it fires up there might be a bit of a kick."

This news alarmed Brody, "What do you mean - kick?"

Harry was sanguine, "Oh, nothing. This cable is connected directly into the school power supply. By my calculations there's enough juice to run the school and get the fusion reaction going, so we should be ok."

"And if we're not OK...?" He had the sudden worrying thought that if something went wrong, tardies and detentions would come thick and fast.

"Well, we might get a kick."

"What kind of a kick?" Brody couldn't hide his concern.

"Well, maybe a power cut. Maybe."

"Jeez, now you tell me, Harry."

"You worry too much, Brody."

He called out to Laura in the room next door.

"OK, Laura - throw that switch."

Laura pushed the lever of the big mains switch up and the low hum of a power transformer under increasing stress in the closet size room, rose in intensity.

Harry seemed just a little anxious as he began to bring the nuclear fusion reactor to life.

At this point the only thing left for Brody to do was to place a handwritten card on the table that read: 'NUCLEAR *FUSION REACTOR - A future of clean energy. Harry Figg, assisted by Brody Boyle; 9th Grade'.*

34

Overhead, the saturated clouds were still holding back. Only the occasional fat raindrop fell like a water bomb splatting onto the ground, leaving a dark wet patch on the grey asphalt.

For some time now, e-scooters had been arriving, buzzing around the school yard, eager for the race. The riders slapped high-fives as they passed.

***

Unnoticed in the excitement, a black SUV slowly reversed into a parking space. A door opened and an elegant female leg stepped out.

One of the water bombs burst on her shoe.

Torres looked down to inspect the wet leather, then tilted her head up to track the source. At first, she saw nothing but blackness. Then the shape of a thunder cloud was revealed by a flicker of lightning deep within its huge volume.

Snake and Baggy were doing a brisk business, selling tickets to riders happy to pay a few dollars to take part. To be one of the cool dudes. Not quite in the Snake Crew but on the fringes. Associated, but risk free.

Tonight, though there was an electrifying frisson of danger. Nobody wanted to be left out.

The riders were not lined up so much as gathered like a swarm. Eager to get on with it.

Finally, Snake addressed the competitors, "OK, does anyone not know where Snake Crew corner is?"

A hand went up.

"Somebody tell him," Snake said. Any other stupid, time-wasting questions?"

A rider asked what the rules were.

"No rules. You get there any way you can."

Snake rode his scooter slowly along the front line of gathered riders, like a general before a battle.

He might have yelled, "Cry Havoc! Let slip the dogs of war." But this wasn't some Shakespearian melodrama.

Instead, he said.

"Now, are those batteries ramped with amps?"

An excited chorus of cheers went up.

"Are your eyes on the prize?"

Another cheer.

"Now, Let's ace this race. Can you losers do that?!"

As one, they all yelled, "Yeah!"

If they had hats, they would have thrown them in the air.

As ready to go as they were, Baggy warned Snake that there were still a few riders that hadn't turned up yet.

"We're good to go," Snake said. "Those jerks are going to miss it and there ain't no refunds."

35

The humming sound had risen to a heavy drone accompanied by the timpani of the vacuum pump hammering away.

The noise was drawing the angry attention of the hydroelectric family. Then the students and visitors at the other tables began raising their irritated voices.

Jarvis arrived to complain, "Can you turn that racket dow..."

His voice was drowned out as the fusion reactor ignited with an explosion of violet radiance and a staccato crackling of static electricity that filled the room.

Anxious eyes turned to see what had happened.

Harry furiously played with the panel to bring it back under control.

Recovering from the shock, Jarvis demanded Harry explain.

"What the hell is that thing?"

Brody handed him the card.

"It's the future - a working fusion reactor," he said, as though such things were a common, everyday experience.

"You brought a fusion reactor into my school. Are you insane?

"Well, it's only a prototype,"

Harry butted in, "But scale it up and yes, this is the future."

Crestfallen by the sudden arrival of a real, functioning exhibit, Jody, the hydroelectric student was no longer quite so smug. She looked dejectedly back and forth between her amateurish model and the impressive reactor. Her indignant parents set off to complain to the principal.

"Let me through." An unexpected but familiar voice. "I need to get through, please."

Brody's mother arrived elbowing her way to the front of the crowd gathered around the reactor. She was accompanied by officer Dave Fiennes, looking cool in his cowboy hat.

Brody assumed the worst.

"Mom!" He said, "Are you in trouble?" She nodded to the man standing next to her.

"Dave? No, he brought me here. As a friend," she assured him.

He stepped forward, took his hat off and swept it over the table full of equipment.

"That's some project you got yourself there, Brody," Dave said. "I am truly impressed."

Rachel turned to the crowd and announced proudly.

"That's my Brody that done that. Always knew he was special."

"Now mom, you know it was Harry, not me."

Rachel wasn't having any of that. She picked up the card.

"Well, the card says you assisted Mr Figg, so you done it too, isn't that right Dave?"

"Anything you say, Rach. – Whatever you say."

36

Outside in the yard, the scooter riders were lined up and impatient to go. Snake checked his watch.

"OK! Are you ready?"

He didn't bother to hold his hand up like a starting flag, that would have put him at a disadvantage. And Snake wasn't the kind of guy who liked being at a disadvantage.

He gripped both handles of his e-scooter and shouted:

"Three... Two... One..."

***

As he yelled, "GO!", somewhere in a school hallway, a hammer smashed the glass of a fire emergency box. The alarm bell rang loud and urgent throughout the building.

That's when the race began.

And the next few drops of rain fell.

***

Snake shot ahead. There was never any doubt that this was a race he was going to win one way or another.

He looked back and smirked at the pack of ordinary, factory equipped scooters trying to catch his special, souped-up ride.

***

Meanwhile, back in the gym, teachers rushed to initiate the school's evacuation procedure. With indignation burning as brightly as the violet star, Principal Jarvis turned to Harry, Brody and Laura with an angry accusation.

"It's that infernal machine!"

He turned to the people gathered in the crowded hall and made an announcement. He had to raise his voice over the noise.

"Can I have your attention everyone. No need to panic. Teachers, remember your fire drill. Open the emergency doors. No running, please. We'll all walk in an orderly fashion out into the schoolyard."

While all this was going on the local news reporter was busy snapping pictures of the mayhem. Jarvis seethed with fury that the pictures won't be celebrating *"Principal Jarvis' proud achievements at Jordon County High"*. Instead, the headline was going to shout: "CATASTROPHE AT COUNTY HIGH."

The principal was a political animal, and in politics it's always someone else's fault: Someone must pay!

Jarvis turned to Brody and Harry again, "You two - my office - first thing tomorrow!"

And, as an after-thought.

"And shut that thing down!"

Officer Fiennes took Brody's mother by the waist and gently escorted her towards the exit.

Outside, the schoolyard was already filling with parents, students and teachers. Some hanging around out of curiosity, others already heading towards their vehicles - and home. They'd had enough.

37

Harry's fusion reactor was still running noisily. The violet light as bright as ever.

"Do you think the reactor's done something, Harry?" Brody asked.

"Set the school on fire?" Laura worried.

"This has nothing to do with the reactor. My guess is, its…"

In the mains supply room, a hand reached for the power switch and slammed it off.

The lights throughout school went out.

"…The Corporation!" Harry said.

The sports hall went dark, except for the eerie iridescence of the star in a jar: it was still busy fusing atoms.

***

Alarm bells were ringing as the dim glow of emergency lighting came on throughout the school.

After calling the emergency services, Principal Jarvis had returned to the gym. The only people still in the building, as far as he knew, were Brody, Laura, Harry.

"Mr Figg. I want you and the students out of the building now. The fire department are on their way." he said.

Harry objected, "But I can't leave..."

"No arguments. Leave that..." he struggled for words, "...that atomic fireball and get out. All of you. NOW!"

It took a few minutes for Harry to power down the reactor. Throwing switches. The turning of controls.

The hall grew darker as the star, still burning in its containment chamber, flickered out. The violet iridescence extinguished. The crackling static, silenced.

A final check and he shepherded Brody and Laura out of the gymnasium, leaving the room empty.

His invention unprotected.

***

With the entire school building to themselves Torres and Roberts crept into the gym, stalked around tables of abandoned science projects, to Harry's experiment.

Torres put her hand tentatively on the containment chamber.

"The core's still warm. Watch out when you disconnect those cables," she warned.

They worked at speed and in silence to get the containment chamber free of cables and pipes. Stopping every now and then to listen for the sound of unwanted company.

***

Outside, Harry, Brody and Laura stood together in the crowded yard. In the distance, they could hear the klaxon of the approaching fire engine.

Harry said, "I can't leave the fusion device unattended. It's those two spies from the Corporation. I bet you a noble gas to an Oganessian atom they have something to do with this calamity."

"An orgasm atom? Wait! What…?" Brody said.

"Element 118," Harry said dismissively. "It's not important. What is important, I've got to get back inside the school."

38

Way behind Snake, the other scooters, riding hard, streaked through the town centre, jumping lights, weaving dangerously around cars and buses, trying to catch up.

On the sidewalk, pedestrians with their eyes fixed to their phones, suddenly found themselves in the middle of a speedway track.

They jumped out of the way as a line of scooters, their electric motors whining at full power, buzzed noisily past like a swarm of bees.

***

It had been a slow day for officer Alison Renfrew as she drove back to the station to sign off her shift.

A few spots of rain splatted her windshield as her mind wandered to thoughts of a chilled-out evening. A bucket of chicken nuggets on her lap as she watched TV. And pretty darned soon too.

That idyllic thought was interrupted by the sudden flash of Snake tearing across a junction against a red light.

A rush of adrenalin brought her quickly back to the present. Alert now and focused, she switched on the lights and gave chase.

Snake was feeling pretty good. Most of the work was done. If the battery held out, he'd be at the Snake Crew club house and counting his winnings in a few minutes.

He snatched another look behind to check he was still clear. Why wouldn't he be – none of the others had the souped-up motor and the high energy, thirty-six-amp-hour battery that his ride had.

At first he thought it was just another lighting flash. What he didn't expect to see were the cops, coming up fast, strobes blazing like a county fairground.

Snake tried to shake his pursuer by veering off into a shopping mall parking lot. He drove up close to the mall entrance and slowed to let the automatic doors opened and let him in. He rode through and stopped to send a smug look to the cop who'd drawn up outside, just as the doors began to close again.

Alison caught the full force of the cocky challenge. She parked, got out and gave chase on foot through the automatic doors, which took an irritating few seconds to open.

Watching the scooter dodge through the shoppers as it sped deep into the mall, two things dawned on Alison: The first, the chicken nuggets would have to wait. And second, there was no way she could catch the offender on foot.

That's when she spotted a line of Segways outside a store.

This was a first for Alison. She could ride a bike. A bike has two wheels. How hard could it be if the wheels, instead of being one in front of the other, were side by side? It looks stupid. There's no way anything can stay upright with such an absurd configuration.

Who the hell thought of that? Well, it was Dean Kamen back at the start of the millennium. Clever guy. But the most insane fact is that Segway Inc was bought by a Brit in two thousand and nine and guess what – he died in two thousand and ten when he fell from a cliff – while riding his Segway.

She grabbed one, turned the power on and released the kickstand. Hesitantly she climbed aboard, aware that this kind of recklessness could result in the sort of comedy act people pay to see when the circus comes to town.

She was surprised to find it balancing despite her wobbling instability. Pushing the control stick seemed to make it go.

It wasn't pretty, but she eventually managed to stay mostly upright as she slowly picked up speed to catch up with her quarry.

The crowds in the mall slowed his escape. But an e-scooter is a nimble thing and Snake slalomed like a professional around sunglasses islands, cell phone huts, network service stands, people and other obstacles - all the time looking back to check his lead over the cop.

39

The fire engine arrived through the gates and parked its huge bulk in the centre of the schoolyard. A couple of firefighters climbed out and Principal Jarvis approached them.

Harry looked on helplessly, "I can't just wait here. I need to get back in.

"Maybe I can get in round the back," Brody suggested.

That bothered Laura, "Be careful Brody."

He was already on his way when the firefighters entered the school through the main doors.

In the gym, Torres and Roberts had stripped sheets of material from other tables and draped it over the core in a futile attempt to hide it.

"Jesus, this thing is heavy," Roberts said as he struggled with his one good arm.

They carried it through the double doors into the corridor. They had nearly reached the rear exit when a youth collided with them.

Roberts snarled, "Look were you're going kid."

"Hey! That's Harry's!" Brody yelled.

He took hold of it with both hands and attempted to wrench it from the thieves. At thirteen, going on fourteen years old he was still some way from the powerful adult he would eventually become. It was no contest. A fight he had no chance of winning.

The spies dropped the device and grabbed Brody and dragged him, shouting and cussing into a nearby janitor's closet. They didn't have a key for the lock, so they heaved a nearby cupboard up against the door. Crude but effective.

With Brody hollering and banging, the spies lifted the reactor core once again and carried it out into the yard where their vehicle was parked. Torres punched the remote. The tailgate rose, and they stowed the core inside.

***

The only good news for Brody was that, in the closet-sized space, he'd found a light switch. The next step was obvious. He reached for his cell phone and tapped a text to Laura.

Outside in the yard, Laura's cell buzzed. She swiped it open and read Brody's message.

"They got the reactor. U gotta stop them. Tell Snake."

No sooner had she read the message than a black SUV glided past. She glanced through the window and saw the containment chamber inside, partially hidden under a cloth. What Laura needed to do now was find Harry and fast.

The school yard was still full of people hanging around. Wanting to see what happens next. Some would deny it but, if the school was going to burn down, they wanted to be there to see it.

Because of the crowd the car was making slow progress threading its way through to the gate. The problem was, the people just weren't in a hurry to get out of the way. And they gave the occupants of the SUV the full extent of their irritation when Torres sounded the horn a couple of times.

Roberts was really getting irate. People were rapping on the windows. Yelling for them to slow down.

"Come on, Torres, stop pussyfooting around. Get us out a here."

***

Inside the school, the fire crew were still checking classrooms and hallways for signs of fire. Nothing yet. Then came shouting and banging. It didn't take long for them to locate the source.

They shifted the cupboard, opened the door and Brody sprang out. He didn't hang around to explain but rushed out into the school yard looking for the SUV.

It hadn't got far.

Without any explanation, Torres stepped on the brake and put the vehicle in 'Park'.

"What the hell are you doing?" Roberts said.

"I just remembered something. Wait here."

She was already out of the vehicle.

"Are you kidding?" Roberts yelled. "We got what we came for."

Torres ignored him and sprinted off, dodging her way through the crowd as she ran back into the school building.

Roberts' difficulties got worse when an angry fire chief came over and indicated Roberts should wind the window down.

"Get this vehicle out of here. It's in the way"

Roberts played for time.

"Yeah, yeah. In a minute, pal."

The fire chief raised the temperature.

"Now! I want this vehicle moved."

With that developing point of contention gathering steam, Brody saw his chance. He sneaked up to the rear of the car and opened the tailgate just enough for him to slide in right next to the core.

Outside, the row between Roberts and the fire chief was still blazing.

The fire chief was adamant.

"First thing. I'm not your pal. Second, I'm about to write you a citation if you don't do as I say and get this thing moved out of the way - now!"

Roberts was stubborn.

"What's your hurry? Where's the fire?"

40

In the dim emergency light, Torres navigated her way around the displays until she reached Harry and Brody's table. It didn't take her long to spot the thing she was looking for. She checked inside the plastic carrier bag and confirmed it had both the laptop and Harry's notes.

Mission complete, she headed for the exit.

Outside, on the steps to the main entrance doors, Harry was trying to persuade the fire fighter standing guard to let him through.

"You don't understand, there's some extremely valuable equipment in there," he said. "It's an emergency."

The fire fighter in full bunker gear, helmet and boots was both a formidable force and an immovable object that Harry couldn't persuade.

"You're gonna have to wait until the chief says it's all clear, sir."

That's when Torres rushed through the doors and crashed into both of them. Harry's first instinct was to apologise to the woman, until a second later when he recognised her.

Then he saw she had his stuff.

"Hey! That's mine!" he shouted as she ran off.

Officer Fiennes heard Harry's cry, looked over, saw the woman running through the crowd and chased after her.

Torres reached the SUV, climbed in and threw the bag with the laptop and notebook onto the back seat.

Roberts was still bickering and seemed ready to step outside and take the fire chief on.

"Give it a rest Roberts."

She shouted an apology.

"Sorry, chief. We're gone."

She didn't wait for an answer. The motor revved angrily and the window wound up cutting the fire chief off. They sped towards the gates.

Dave Fiennes sprinted up to the chief. They both watched the vehicle drive away. The chief wasn't happy.

"Assholes."

Dave nodded an agreement. Then Brody's head appeared in the rear window and gave him a wave.

"Oh jeez. That's not good." Dave said.

He hurried back to Rachel and didn't notice the SUV take a left turn at the school gates.

"I've got to go, Rach. I just saw Brody. He snuck in the back of the car with those villains. They're heading out of the yard."

Harry said, "I'm coming with you. They've stolen my reactor core."

"You're not going anywhere without me," Rachel declared. "That's my son in there."

All three climb into Dave's police cruiser, Rachel in front, Harry in back. He switched on the bar lights, turned right out of the school gates and gave chase – in the wrong direction.

41

Somehow, Laura had got left behind. She watched helplessly as the police car drove off without her.

At the same time waiter Steve rode into the yard on an e-scooter and pulled up next to her.

"Have I missed it?" Steve asked.

"What?"

"You know. The race? I got held up at Jake's."

"Yeah, they've gone." Then another option occurred to her. "Wait a minute. Get off."

"What?"

Laura was already pulling on the handlebars, "I need your scooter."

"I'm not giving you my scooter," Steve said defiantly.

Laura went for his weak spot.

"Come on Steve," she said softly in his ear. "You'll do it for me won't you. That's what you told me. And I'd do anything for you, Steve."

Steve was weakening, "Well, I don't know..."

Laura was in a hurry.

"Steve, get off the damn scooter," she shouted. "NOW!"

Riding an e-scooter for the first time, Laura pulled to a stop at the school gates and turned left - in the direction of Snake Crew HQ.

Above her another brilliant display of lightning cascaded across the sky.

***

The chase in the shopping mall had been ongoing for a while. The speed of the Segway increased in direct proportion to Alison's confidence. Sometimes she could even see Snake bobbing and weaving ahead as shoppers parted to let him through.

There was a real chance that she could catch up if she just had the courage to push the stick forward a little more. The machine picked up speed. She was barely in control.

A child ran out of the Disney Store. She swerved, and that's all it took.

It was a nasty fall. Sliding to a stop outside a pet food store with one unlucky customer taking a tumble with her. Alison groaned as she stood up. She apologised to the woman and helped her gather her shopping.

"Sorry mam. Police business. Trying to catch a kid who jumped some lights."

The lady had nothing pleasant to say.

"Then why aren't you out there in the street arresting him instead of playing games in the mall."

It might have irritated Alison if she wasn't already heading back to her car.

At the mall's south exit, Snake crept through the doors. He looked back to see if he was still being chased, twisted the accelerator handle and escaped into the night. He still had the edge. Despite the time-wasting detour, he could still win.

***

Fiennes cruiser had slowed so they could check the side roads they passed.

"Are you sure they went this way?" Fiennes wondered.

Harry commented from the back, "How about you use the radio? That's what they do on TV."

Fiennes reached for the handset, "Officer Renfrew? Alison? It's Dave."

A familiar voice replied, "How's it hanging Dave?"

"There's been a robbery at the school. Perps got away in a black SUV." He gave her the plate number.

Outside the mall, Alison was standing next to her police cruiser, the radio mic in her hand.

"Copy that. Just chased that McKay kid on an electric scooter riding like a bat through the mall..."

Back in Fiennes' car they heard Alison say, "Wait a minute..."

Radio hash filled the silence followed by a 'click' as the mic came on again.

"Well, there's something you don't see every day. A bunch of electric scooters just raced past. They sure are in a hurry. Better go. I'll look out for that SUV."

The transmission ended abruptly.

"Well, looks like Alison's got her hands full. Maybe we should head back."

Fiennes spun the wheel for a hard one hundred and eighty turn.

***

Alison had caught up with the scooter pack and began chasing them through the city centre, red and blues flashing. They didn't seem to be paying attention so she gave the siren a couple of 'whoops'.

Two scooters peeled off into a side road. Renfrew ignored them and stayed with the larger group as they raced over a red light at a four-way junction.

Back in the SUV, Torres was approaching the same junction. She was clear to cross on green but the peloton of scooters cutting across forced her to brake hard.

Chasing the scooters just a few yards behind, Alison had nowhere to go - except straight into Torres' fender.

In the back, Brody was shaken but unharmed by the crash. He peeked over the seat to see what had happened.

The SUV was damaged but drivable. Torres touched the accelerator and the car lumbered noisily across the junction, the damaged fender rubbing against the tyre. She ignored the sound, revved harder and disappeared from sight.

She left behind a shocked but recovering Officer Renfrew in her damaged police car. The motor had stalled. She gave the starter button another press.

Nothing.

"Shoot!"

She reached for the radio handset.

"You there, Dave? Just seen your SUV."

There was some radio hash, then, "Do tell."

"Well, after it took my car out it took off west, through the old town."

"Ouch! You OK, Alison?"

"Yeah. Looks like I'm going to have to walk home, though."

"Old town, west, you say?"

"Copy that," Alison confirmed. "They have some damage. Might slow them down."

Alison got out to check the damage to her car.

42

It was a poorly lit stretch of road that led to the outskirts of town. The city limits are where all industry and commerce get shoved, no matter where the town, no matter what the country. The commercial parks, the industrial estates - the ugly stuff no one wants to live near is always on the edge of town.

One headlight was out. The hood was buckled and the fender rubbed against the front wheel. Steering was difficult and the motor was making a strange noise. The only thing that worked were the windshield wipers, automatically clearing the drops that had started to hit the glass in increasing numbers.

"See if you can fix that fender." Torres said.

"What, with my one arm?"

Torres played the weak female gambit, "You're a guy. You can do guy stuff, even with one arm." She practically batted her eyelids.

The SUV pulled over.

Roberts was suspicious but got out and took a look at the damage. He got a grip on the bent metal and tried to pull the fender off of the wheel with one hand.

"I need a tyre lever," he shouted to Torres.

He went to the back of the car and reached for the button to open the tailgate.

Inside, Brody realised with horror he was about to be exposed. He got ready to leap out and run.

Before Roberts' finger could touch the button, to his slack-jawed shock, the vehicle drove off – without him.

He stood there in the smoke and dust as the vehicle sped away, with the face of a boy staring back at him through the rear window.

***

Riding fast - throttle wide open, Laura felt her cell phone vibrate. She pulled it out and saw a message from Brody, "*I'm in the SUV. Where's Snake?*"

She replaced the cell in her jacket and wiped away the rain that blurred her vision. She couldn't reply right now. He'd just have to wait.

43

When Baggy arrived at the lot, Snake was leaning through the van door sheltering from the weather as he counted the cash onto the footwell.

They fist bumped each other.

"Sick!" Baggy said.

"Like I told you, Bags. With the souped-up motors and bigger batteries we couldn't lose."

"Easy money," Baggy boasted.

"Yeah, and plenty of it," Snake said as he fanned out the bills for Baggy to see.

***

In the back of the SUV Brody listened as Torres made a call.

"I'm solo and the package is onboard. Do we still have a deal, Larson?"

A foreign sounding voice replied.

"Just get it to the old warehouse as arranged. Ten minutes."

The call ended abruptly.

Torres muttered to herself, "Don't try to screw me, Larson."

After overhearing the conversation, Brody sent another message.

***

At the corner lot, more riders had arrived and were gathered around the old club house van to moan and bitch to Snake about being cheated.

Unsympathetic as always, Snake saw it differently.

"Yeah, well grow up, or go complain to your mothers."

He looked up at the sound of a late arrival swerving onto the stoney wasteland in a big hurry and an urgent message.

"Snake! Brody needs your help." Laura called out breathlessly as she skidded to a halt.

She turned to the other riders.

"Guys. Everyone! Brody's in trouble. He needs your help."

"I'm busy," Snake said. "Tell him to ask those three French guys."

Snake's response threw Laura.

"What French guys?"

She tried again, "Come on Snake, those Corporation spies stole Harry's fusion reactor thing and now they've got Brody."

Snake wasn't interested. He turned his back and continued counting his and Baggy's share of the cash on the rusty floor of the van.

She turned to the other two Snake Crew gang members.

"Baggy. Lloyd. You guys are Brody's friends," she pleaded. "Look, I know where they're going."

She held out her cell phone with Brody's last message.

"See? That old warehouse. Just out of town? They're meeting some guy there. That's where Brody will be. We've got to go. Now!"

Baggy was reluctant, "I'm not sure there's enough juice in the tank, Laura."

But Lloyd came through for her, "Well, we won't know till we try. Come on Bags."

He turned to the others.

"How about it guys? Come on – Brody needs us."

Embarrassed muttering came from reluctant riders.

"Well, I don' know. I gotta head home. Looks like rain."

Lloyd said, "Well, there's nothing on TV, so what the hell."

Lloyd raced off at high speed. Baggy followed, leading the posse riding hard to catch up. That left Snake, back at the ranch, stubbornly counting the cash.

Snake looked over to Laura and caught her angry glare. He tried to swagger it out.

"Don't give me that look. Brody can take care of himself. And anyway, I'm busy here."

"Yeah, busy taking care of Peter 'Snake' McKay." She said scornfully.

She punched out another text to Brody.

"*We're coming. Keep your head down.*"

And took off after the others.

Brody read the message from Laura then sneaked a quick look.

They were approaching the warehouse.

44

The road out of town was mostly deserted at this time of night. All the industrial and commercial toing and froing was done. The day's business, over.

Just one lonely figure stood by a streetlamp, his collar up against the increasingly worsening weather. He was on the phone to The Corporation.

"Yeah, she sold out. I don't think she'll get far - we nearly totalled the car."

A pause as he listened.

"That's not fair. I didn't see it coming. She played me. She played all of us."

Out of the dark, with the sound of high revving electric motors and the rush of wind, the scooters raced past Roberts.

He turned at the sudden sound and watched them disappear down the road.

Overhead, lighting streaked across the sky shaking lose more huge drops of rain.

"I'm guessing she may have company soon."

***

Fast and urgent, Baggy and Lloyd lead the squadron of scooters on their mission to rescue Brody. They lost one rider when his battery gave out. It was a worrying sign that others might not make it either.

Laura was still grappling with the novelty of e-scooter riding and was some distance behind when she came upon the forlorn figure of the boy pushing his scooter.

"We'll catch you on the way back." She shouted as she flew past.

He waved at the receding figure, turned, and continued his lonely trek back into town.

***

Like huge Jurassic bones lying abandoned amid the economic wilderness and industrial decay of the town's business park, the pile of rotting steel and brick that remained of the old warehouse was a miserable reminder of happier times when full employment meant mortgages could be paid and vacations enjoyed.

It had a large concrete apron that butted right against the road that Torres had arrived on. Moments later she watched as Larson's Ford Explorer drove in and stopped twenty feet away. Its headlights played on the gloomy hulk silhouetted against the blackness of the Jordan County landscape.

Torres got out, locked the car with the remote and approached the Ford. She stopped a few yards back and waited.

Wearing a grey suit, white shirt, no tie, Larson, a blonde six-footer from Scandinavia stepped out of the Ford and waited too. With his ice blue eyes, he was like an over-exposed picture. No contrast. Almost albino.

Torres figured he might be Swedish, or maybe Norwegian. She went with Swedish. His driver-henchman stayed at the wheel.

A sudden squall whipped up by a gust of wind sprayed rain across the parking lot. Torres wiped the moisture from her face with the back of her hand.

The two of them looked at each other like gunslingers in a main street shoot out.

As though to dramatize the moment, a jagged fork of lightning speared across the sky. A loud roll of thunder followed almost immediately.

Torres drew first. "The money?"

"The core," Larson countered. "I think I should see that first. That seems fair, doesn't it?"

Torres gave that option some thought, then led him over to the SUV.

Seeing the two approaching, Brody had scrambled over the back of the rear seats and squeezed down into the foot well by the time they arrived. That's when he spotted the shopping bag.

Outside, Torres used the remote and swung the tailgate up to show Larson the fusion reactor.

"That's it. You're going to have to take my word that it works."

She slammed the gate and locked the car once again with the remote.

"So, the money?"

Larson grunted something in Swedish that sounded like grudging agreement.

As they walked back to his Explorer she said, "I also have the laptop and notebook. You'll need both."

Another grunt from Larson.

The silence was suddenly broken by Torres' car alarm bursting into deafening life. They turned to look and saw the figure of a boy caught in the flashes of the orange signal lights. He was on the run with the plastic shopping bag.

"The kid's got the laptop! Stop him!" she yelled.

Larson signalled his henchman and all three chased after Brody, fanning out to head him off.

***

Along the deserted strip of road, it was strange to find a man standing alone. Dave Fiennes pulled up alongside and wound the passenger window down.

"We're looking for a black SUV that was last seen heading this way?"

Roberts played dumb, "SUV?" He shook his head.

Harry thought he recognised him – it was difficult to tell in the dark.

He whispered to Fiennes. "I think that's one of them."

Fiennes got out and walked around to the stranger. The rain was still holding off, mostly. It came in tentative handfuls of fat drops thrown randomly by a capricious wind.

"That SUV? You sure you haven't seen it?"

"Wait a minute. Yeah. Went past a while ago," Roberts said. He nodded west in the out-of-town direction.

Dave took his hat off, scratched his head thoughtfully and slipped it back on as another few wet drops hit him.

He gave Roberts a hard look.

"What were you doing at the school earlier - you know anything about a robbery?"

Roberts played it cool, "You've got it wrong deputy. I'm just hitching through."

"We'll see about that."

With his hand ready on his holster, he reached for the handcuffs clipped to his belt.

"Let's see those hands - now!"

Fiennes cuffed Roberts and pushed him into the rear seat next to Harry, just as Laura arrived on the scooter.

She looked in and saw Rachel.

"Oh, Hi Mrs Boyle. I know where Brody is."

She looked over to Fiennes who was just closing the rear passenger door.

"The old warehouse. You've got to hurry."

"That's where we're heading," Dave said. "Let's put your scooter in the back, Laura, and you can squeeze in next to Harry."

It was a struggle but she and Dave managed to jam the scooter into the trunk.

She shimmied into the cruiser next to Harry.

"Hi Harry."

"Hi Laura," he said glumly.

Dave put his foot down and sped off, strobes blazing.

Laura stared past Harry to the prisoner.

"Who's your friend Harry?"

"Just some loser we picked up."

45

Overhead, the storm coming up from the south that had been threatening all afternoon was finally about to land; the energy in those weather cells born in the Gulf of Mexico could really pack a punch.

The squadron of scooters tore noisily onto the warehouse concourse and circled the enemy just as Larson's henchman was closing in on Brody.

Apart from lightning, the only illumination came from the headlamps of the two vehicles and the red scooter taillights flitting around like a swarm of fireflies in the humid air.

Even though Brody and his pursuers were just shadowy shapes, Baggy quickly picked his friend out. It took some skilful swerving manoeuvres to avoid the villains, but he finally came alongside.

"Brody! Get on!"

Baggy grabbed hold of the boy as he ran and barely managed to keep the machine under control as the teenager leaped on board.

"I got a message from Laura. She's on her way with the cops," Brody shouted over the rumble of thunder. "Any time now."

The three villains were on foot in the increasingly persistent rain and being harried by the other scooter riders, keeping them busy while the two boys got away.

Baggy's souped-up machine soon had the edge on the villains. It didn't take long. They drove through a broken doorway into the uncertain safety of the derelict warehouse.

Outside, in the deluge, the scooters were still at it. Soaked to the skin and taking big risks. Spectacular crashes took a couple of riders out when their scooters careened across the wet concrete in a shower of sparks.

In what seemed like a futile kamikaze stunt, Lloyd aimed for the henchman and successfully knocked him flying into the pooling water. He almost took himself out at the same time. Luck and some skill kept him upright.

That's when the game suddenly got serious.
The goon got to his feet, pulled a gun from his belt and fired several shots in the air.

That got the young riders' attention. They hadn't seen it coming. It had been fun up until then. Like a cop show or something on TV – not real.

Most hadn't heard the sound of real handgun fire before but they instinctively knew that the series of loud bangs represented danger!

Fear for their lives drove them at high speed towards the warehouse.

The crooks followed them in.

***

Inside it was dark and forbidding. The only light came from the Ford Explorer's headlamps shining like laser beams through slits in boarded windows, cracks in vandalised service doors and gaps in the crumbling masonry.

The space was cluttered with abandoned packing cases, shipping containers, rusting machinery and random junk that formed alleyways and rat runs. That it was mostly dry was the only up-side.

Outside the storm had broken. And it was one for the books. Lighting was strobing endlessly across the sky, rolling thunder shook the fragile old structure and rain, driven by whistling storm-force squalls, penetrated the roof. The asphalt roofing material had cracked and degraded years ago and now torrents of water began cascading to the concrete floor thirty meters below like rain forest waterfalls.

Baggy hid Brody behind an old iron staircase that had intricately patterned cast-iron steps. Brody looked up and saw that it spiralled up to a gantry running the length of the building.

"Stay here - keep your head down," Baggy said.

He motored away and joined the other kids who had made it into the warehouse.

The plan was to play a game of cat and mouse - taking it in turns to carry an extra rider in the hope that, in the dark, the villains would think it was Brody. A diversion they hoped would keep Brody safe until the cops arrived.

It almost worked, until Torres, Larson and the henchman came up with a plan of their own. And it wasn't subtle.

They strew boxes and junk across the narrow alleyway. That brought most of the scooters down. The henchman took the last of the vinegar out of them. A couple of rounds from his Glock 17 and their youthful enthusiasm quickly faded.

They kettled the ones they caught in a cul de sac of machinery and containers, like cattle in a corral.

Lloyd and Baggy managed to keep clear of the danger for a little longer. They'd ridden to the far end of building to get away from trouble. Using their cell phone flashlights, they had a brief parley.

Some might call it a reality check.

"This isn't fun anymore, Baggy," Lloyd said. "Those are seriously mean dudes. What the hell has old Figgy got that those bozo's want?"

"And why are they after Brody?" Baggy added. "What's in that bag?"

Lloyd said, "They've got guns, Baggs. It's all just too real."

"Maybe we better split up," Baggy said. "I'll take that far wall. There might be a way out."

"OK," Lloyd agreed. "I better go check on Brody first."

They took it slow and quietly. In the dark it was a dangerous place to ride around at high speed. And anyway, the three gangsters were still out there - somewhere.

46

He'd been waiting for a while behind the stairs and the buzz of e-scooters had ceased. So too had the voices calling out to him. Telling him to come out. To give himself up.

Something was up.

Still gripping the plastic carrier bag, Brody saw his chance. He began climbing the spiral stairway towards the gantry high above. It soon became clear that this might not have been the safest choice. Many steps were missing. Others fixed in place with just a single bolt. Great lengths of the handrail itself was missing or hanging off.

To make matters worse, a stream of rainwater was pouring down the steps like river rapids.

The whole structure was a death trap.

Far below, Larson looked up and spotted the shadowy figure of Brody struggling up towards the gantry. He started after him.

Lloyd rode up to the foot of the stairs, saw Brody high above, but alarmingly, not far below, one of the gangsters climbing towards him, grim and determined.

The drama playing out above absorbed him so completely that he jumped with shock when a hand grabbed his shoulder. He turned. It was the woman. Lloyd hadn't had a long life but in his young opinion this was a lady who looked like she could handle herself.

"You're done here," Torres said. "Let's go."

She led him away to join the others.

***

The old iron stairs, weakened with age, started to sag and sway under the strain of Larson's extra weight. Terrified by the sudden movement, Brody froze. Then he heard a voice shouting up to him.

"Kid! I only want the bag. Just leave it on the step and move away."

He looked down and was horrified to see in the flickering lightning, a gangster, just one full turn of the staircase below.

The sight of Larson made him even more determined. He fought his anxiety, made worse by the nerve-shredding squeal of tortured metal as the staircase swayed, and climbed faster. He used the loose handrail as leverage but it broke away, nearly taking him with it as the metal work tumbled and clanged against the iron structure on its way to the ground.

His foot tested each cast iron step before putting his weight on it. Three were missing near the top. He gripped the vertical steel posts that had once supported the handrail and started to inch his way around the gap using the thin iron frame on the side. He could only get so far because the steel uprights ran out. There were more on the other side but stretching his leg across the vertical drop left his toes barely touching the metalwork. He was in danger of toppling. With only the tips of his fingers gripping a post, he swung himself across, pausing for a moment to steady his nerves before attempting the last few feet.

The gantry itself was just one step away. His means of escape to what he hoped would be safety. Once across he could run the length of it to reach the stairs at the far end and out into the darkness, away from the warehouse and the villains chasing him.

But right now, his problem was Larson, just a few steps below and getting closer.

"You can't get away, kid. You're a brave lad, but you don't have a chance. Leave the bag and go home."

His words were almost drowned by an explosion of thunder that shook the structure like an earthquake.

The storm was now directly overhead. Outside, lightning blazed from horizon to horizon. Shafts of flickering light from the strobing plasma speared through cracks and holes in the roof, lighting the warehouse like a laser show in a New York night club.

Looking across to the gantry, Brody saw it was going to get a lot tougher. An entire section of steel floor grating was missing leaving a huge gap and a sixty-foot drop.

Standing on the last step, Brody braced himself. He leaned into the jump a couple of times, testing his resolve. Finding the courage.

As he was about to leap, the entire staircase shifted sideways when Larson jumped over the missing stair steps. The villain was just half a turn away.

He had nothing to lose. Brody threw himself across the void. The whole structure swung wildly as he landed. The sound of more loose metal braking away added to the cacophony of noise from the storm.

He took a breath. Then he took a step. All seemed calm until, with a groan, the gantry shuddered when a vertical support broke away from its corroded mooring in the roof.

Clinging to the handrail, he inched carefully along. He seemed to be making progress at last until he was knocked off his feet when Larson made the same leap across to the gantry.

The extra weight was too much for the frail ironwork. Both Larson and Brody were thrown in the air as the gantry dropped several feet beneath them. Steel debris fell to the ground in a bone shaking crash that shook the scooter kids watching their friend as he clung to the swaying structure high above.

He'd made it to the gantry but for the young teenager it was now a dangerous uphill climb. A look behind showed the Swede was slowly but doggedly inching his way across the treacherous walkway. He was going to reach him soon if he didn't get a move on.

Larson called out again, "What's your name, boy?"

Nothing from Brody. His name was his business.

"You're risking your life for nothing, boy. Just slide the bag down to me."

"No way. You're just going to have to take it."

Brody climbed faster. Taking less care. Ahead, but still some distance away, were the concrete stairs that the gantry was attached to. With the ironwork swinging and shuddering, and the metal fixings bending and twisting the ancient partnership between concrete and steel was likely to end pretty soon.

Like an acrobat high in the roof of a big top, his escape along the weakening structure was becoming even riskier, with the added pressure of Larson just yards behind him.

Far below, the teenagers watched in open-mouthed terror. Some called up to encourage him, but others shouted courage sapping words of despair.

"Give up Brody – it just isn't worth it."

Larson used those voices against him.

"So, it's Brody. That's a cool name."

Patronising Brody wasn't going to work. He continued the treacherous climb towards the stairs.

"You see, Brody, even your friends are telling you to give up," he shouted across to him. "This isn't your fight. I only want the bag."

Brody's resolve hardened. He didn't bother to reply.

Still free and hidden in the darkness, Baggy shouted up to him.

"You're doin' great Brody boy. You ain't got far to go. Don't let the son of a bitch get you."

That loud call of support brought Baggy's freedom to an end. He felt the barrel of a gun thrust hard into his back as the henchman dragged him off to join his friends in the corral.

47

He was closer now.

Another stretch of missing walkway grating forced him to crab along the narrow side girder. His fingers reaching for any part of the structure that seemed secure. Though there was little he would trust with his life.

The safety of the concrete stairs lay just ahead. His arm stretched out to the vertical rungs that surrounded the landing like a rotting picket fence.

Suddenly, with a terrible groan of tortured steel, the gantry gave way on one side and rotated a precarious ninety degrees.

His fingers missed the handrail as the structure swung from under him. His fall was broken by a bruising impact on a section of twisted steel. Below him was the yawning abyss of a fifty-foot drop.

His friends watched Brody swinging one-handed, high above them. Even Torres looked worried.

The ironwork screeched and creaked and the remaining bolts started to bend and tear loose as Larson clawed his way up the wreckage towards the stairs.

Taking a firm hand hold, Larson looked down at the boy clinging to the scrap of iron like a survivor of a ship wreck. He still had the bag in his free hand.

"I'll make you a deal," he said.

Brody was tiring quickly.

It was a cruel bargain.

"The bag first, then I give you my hand."

Brody had no choice. He handed the bag up to the gangster. Larson put it to one side and reached down. He grasped Brody's wrist and pulled hard.

"You're heavier than you look," Larson said. "I can't do this on my own. You're going to have to put some effort into it."

Not being particularly athletic, Brody struggled but eventually managed to swing his feet up and get a foothold on a girder. Even so, Larson was tiring quickly. It took a strength sapping final effort to pull the boy up.

Brody didn't wait to recover, he climbed over Larson and, with the last of his strength, sprung over to the concrete platform.

He watched Larson pick his way around the twisted ironwork.

"What, you're not going to thank me, Brody?" Larson called sardonically as he climbed. "You could have fallen to certain death and all for nothing. This is how it was always going to end."

What Brody needed was the bag with the laptop and notebook. He wasn't sure how he could persuade Larson to give it to him.

As the Swede drew nearer, gravity provided the answer.

His weight was too much for the rotten bolts and rusting welds that held the gantry to the platform. As he attempted to jump, the whole structure gave way, crashing noisily to the ground, leaving just a frame of loose angle iron for Larson to cling to.

The stakes were now reversed. He offered his hand up to Brody.

"Come on kid," he said. "Help me out here."

"The bag first."

A weld gave way leaving the girder swinging by a single rusty bolt. The jolt nearly dislodged Larson. He had no choice. He passed the bag up to Brody.

Brody hooked his legs through the bars of the railings, giving him the leverage to help Larson up. They both lay on the platform panting from exhaustion.

It was all over pretty quickly.

Breathing heavily, Brody dragged himself up, exhausted, but more importantly, still in possession of the bag. He ran for the stairs.

He was only a couple of steps down when Larson pulled the Glock from his belt and fired a couple of shots into the air.

That stopped Brody dead.

"That's two for free. The next one's for you."

Brody turned and saw the gun pointing at him.

"I'll take that,".

Game over.

He shouted down to Torres and the henchman.

"I've got the bag. Get those kids outside and hold them there."

48

"Switch that noise off!" the henchman shouted to Torres as he herded the boys out onto the forecourt. Torres used her remote to silence the SUV's car alarm.

Like wretched prisoners of war, the teenagers were lined up with their scooters in front of the Ford Explorer. It's headlights casting a harsh light over the sorry group of school kids.

The storm had eased; they pass as quickly as they come. The deluge had reduced to the occasional bloated drop of rain. Lightning still flickered on the horizon but above, stars twinkled intermittently. Even the moon managed to form a hazy yellow shape behind the scudding clouds.

The kids were muttering angry complaints about how they knew their rights, and "You assholes aren't going to get away with it."

One brave soul threatened to walk away,

"What are you going to do, shoot me?"

The henchman grabbed the kid's arm, squeezed and got a pleasing yelp of pain. He pushed his Glock 17 hard against the boys head.

"Anyone else got a complaint?"

Silence.

"You stand there. And you shut up."

They quietened down into sullen obedience.

Shortly after, Larson dragged Brody out of the warehouse to join them.

"You," he said to his driver-henchman. "Go with the woman and get the reactor."

He had Brody's arm in a painful grip as he swept his gun along the row of school kids.

"You came to rescue your friend," Larson said and gave Brody a mean jerk. "I respect your foolish bravery but what did you think you could do with those stupid toys?"

He kicked one of the scooters.

"It's over. Keep quiet and you can go home soon."

Then he turned the weapon on Brody.

"As for you, kid. You've given me enough trouble already."

A distant sound caused Brody to glance over at something beyond the parking lot. Whatever it was, it was hidden behind the brilliance of the one remaining headlight of Torres' SUV.

With then tailgate open, Torres and the henchman were struggling to lift the reactor. Its awkward shape made it hard to get a handhold on.

The Swede was enjoying himself, tormenting the kids and threatening Brody.

"I haven't got time to screw around. How about I just shoot your friend right now?! Is that how you saw this going down?"

He pulled the slide mechanism and held the gun to the teenager's head. Brody felt the cold steel of the barrel pressing hard and painful, but his stubborn streak denied Larson the pleasure of a cry or a whimper. He just stood firm and looked the man in the eye. Tragically, throughout his short life, bullying was something he'd had to get used to.

The other kids though reacted as expected, pleading for Brody's life.

Torres heard the cries and looked over.

"No, Larson! Jesus. Are you kidding?"

"Shut the hell up," Larson yelled back. "And get that thing over here. Quickly."

The humming sound coming out of the dark got the kids attention. Maybe it was their young ears, still fresh and new. Brody heard it too. It wasn't just the hum – there was a buzz, like tyres on concrete. Little wheels, spinning fast.

Their hearing hadn't been softened by years of noise and clutter like Larsons or the other adults.

"Say goodbye to your friend's, Brody," he threatened cruelly.

Then, when it was loud enough, he heard the noise too. He looked up.

Somewhere, beyond Torres' SUV, someone screamed a rebel yell.

"Yaaahooo..."

"What the...!" Larson still couldn't make out what was happening.

Then he could. Too late!

Suddenly, out of the glare of the headlight, an e-scooter came charging towards him like a train.

There was no time to react. It hit him at high speed, throwing him to the ground and hurling the rider over the handlebars, head-first onto the deck.

Snake McKay lifted his head once, then fell back unconscious.

Shouts and cheers erupted from the scooter kids.

Baggy couldn't contain his surprise, "Hey Snake! Where did you come from?"

Lloyd expressed himself in his usual way, "Dope!"

Brody whispered a breathless, "Sick!"

Snake heard none of it.

Flashing lights added to the mayhem as Fiennes' police car skidded to a halt. He threw the door open and leapt out, weapon raised from a crouched position.

As dazed as he was, Larson attempted to reach for his gun lying a few feet away.

"I wouldn't do that. Back away," Dave said.

He swivelled to the henchman who attempted to reach behind his back for his own gun tucked in his belt. But the heavy reactor core he and Torres were trying to lift just got in the way.

"Throw the weapon on the ground," Dave Fiennes said. "Toward me."

The goon did as he was told but he still looked dangerous.

Fiennes stood up and walked carefully towards him.

"You two. Put that thing down," he said. "I need both of you over there with your friend."

They left the reactor and walked over to join Larson.

With his gun ready and his eyes focused on the three villains, Fiennes made a call on his radio.

"I'm going to need urgent back up and paramedics out at the warehouse beyond old town."

A small metallic voice confirmed the request, "Copy that."

Laura had run over to Brody who was tending to Snake.

"Well, this guy is full of surprises," she said as she knelt down.

A moan from Snake as he regained conscious.
"Hey Brody boy."
"Hey Snake," Brody said.

***

Harry and Rachel stepped out of the police cruiser. The old inventor went over to check on his precious reactor.

Brody's mom called out,

"Brody! Brody! Are you OK?" as she ran over to her son. Then came the scolding, "What the hell were you thinking? Doing something stupid like that?"

Brody stood up.

"I guess I wasn't thinking mom. I just. Well I..."

His mother hugged him tightly.

"You just did what you thought you had to. But if you do it again..."

"Yes, Mom."

***

Harry was inspecting the reactor as more police vehicles arrived, lights flashing. A medic ran over to attend to Snake. He had made it to a sitting position.

With the help of another officer, Dave Fiennes was cuffing Larson. At the same time, Torres was balling Larson out.

"You were going to shoot a child?"

He didn't reply and anyway she didn't wait for an answer. Amid the confusion, Torres made a break for it.

She grabbed one of the scooters, got on board, revved hard, and took off at high speed in the direction of the highway.

As she passed Dave Fiennes police car the rear door swung open. She slammed into it face first and cartwheeled to the ground.

Roberts leant out.

"If I'm going down, so are you, Torres."

While Fiennes was leading the villains away, he looked over to Rachel. She looked up. He sent her a smile. She sent one back.

***

"Is it OK, Harry?" Brody said as he ambled over to Harry.

"I don't think there's any permanent damage," he said. "We'll know when we get it back to my workshop."

Brody handed Harry the shopping bag.

"You're going to have to take better care of this stuff, Harry. You know - get some security?"

Harry was already back in a world of his own.

"Hmm, maybe I can do better than that," he mumbled to himself.

49

"You sure Harry won't mind us just walking in like this?"

It was early evening and the unmistakable humming sound could be heard coming from Harry's workshop as Brody and Laura climbed the stairs.

"Naa, it's cool," Brody said.

They stood by the open door and peered in. Something was wrong. Someone was under the desk fiddling with the device and it didn't look like Harry.

"Hey! You! You stealing Harry's stuff?" Brody demanded.

The man stopped what he was doing, twisted awkwardly around and peered from under the work bench to see who had entered the room.

He held his hands up to calm the visitors.

"No, no, it's not like that...," the stranger said, his words spiced with an Indian accent.

He unfolded from under the bench and stood up to his full skinny six-foot, towering over the teenagers in his crumpled jeans that didn't quite meet his scuffed loafers. Despite his height, he didn't appear threatening and the tension eased a little.

That's when Harry entered carrying Schrodinger.

"Oh, you've met Dev."

Brody turned to Harry.

"You know this guy? We thought he was - you know..." Brody didn't quite finish the thought.

"I took your advice," Harry said. "But I needed more than security. I needed a partner. MIT had been in touch."

He held up the letter, now removed from the envelope that had been lying on his work bench for the past couple of weeks.

"So, I got back to them. You know, what with all that happened recently."

"Ah, so you must be Brody," the stranger said. "Harry told me about you. I'm Dr. Dev Anand. Plasma physics at the Massachusetts Institute of Technology," he revealed. "I'm going to be working with Harry."

As Harry reached over to flick some switches the cat leaped from his arms and scampered out of the room. It turned and gave Harry a scathing glare from the hallway.

Harry continued firing up the equipment. Getting those atoms ready to start fusing.

"I was thinking, Dev, we should keep the atomic boundary below 5000 electron volts," Harry said as he worked. "We need higher densities that will keep the nuclei confined for longer. The electric force keeps proton particles apart but the wavefunction allows uncertainty at a quantum level."

The star in a jar flashed on and emitted its brilliant violet light.

Dr. Dev couldn't hide his admiration.

"That really is something Harry. It never fails to astonish me," he said. "It's revolutionary. The guys back at MIT aren't going to believe it till they see it."

An elderly voice called from the hall. They all turned round to see Harry's mom standing in the doorway with Schrodinger brushing against her legs.

"It's nice to see you with all your friend's round. Now tell me - which one of you is Harry?"

She had an interesting range of choices lined up to pick from.

"Mom, how'd you like to live in Massachusetts?" Harry ventured. "They say it's nice this time of year."

"I'm going to miss you Harry," Brody said.

Laura took Brody's hand.

"We're both going to miss you, Harry." she said.

Harry found himself touched by an unfamiliar but unexpectedly pleasant emotion.

"Don't worry, we'll keep in touch. Maybe you'd like to visit? That'd be OK wouldn't it, Dev?"

Doctor Anand was quick to reassure Harry and the two students.

"Absolutely. We're always looking for future quantum physicists."

While Dev looked on, Harry continued to play with the controls, making fine adjustments. The droning noise suddenly dipped momentarily as though under some kind of strain. The overhead lamp flickered.

That's when the neighborhood power went out again.

The workshop was bathed in the violet glow of the nuclear fusion reactor as Harry and Dev walked over to the window.

"Yeah - that's still a problem," Harry said.

Brody and Laura stood there watching the containment chamber. Their faces illuminated by the flickering violet light from the star in a jar.

"That's some weird science, Brody," Laura said.

"No," Brody assured her. "It's just a star called Laura."

***

High above the town suburbs, the neighborhood around Harry's house grew dark as one at a time the lights in the streets and houses nearby started to flicker out.

It was a clear night and with no light pollution, the Milky Way galaxy with its billions of stars flowed across the heavens like a river of silver.

Far below, all that could be seen was a brilliant streak of violet starlight coming from Harry's window.

The End

ACKNOWLEDGEMENTS

FUSORS – THE STAR IN A JAR

The Half Life of Harry Figg is a work of science fiction that I hope you enjoyed. It was originally written as a screenplay that won many awards, including finalist in the Geneva Science in Fiction Screenplay Awards, an honour I am most proud of.

I'm still waiting for a producer to call. It would make an entertaining movie.

You might think that creating fusion in a back bedroom or basement the way Harry Figg does is an outrageous fantasy that stretches your suspension of disbelief to breaking point. But I'm about to surprise you.

I came across the business of stars in jars quite by accident some years ago. Harry Figg's fusion device is of course a work of fiction, but it's based on, and has taken huge liberties with, an existing experimental technology that is unexpectedly accessible to mere mortals like you and me.

Hidden among us is a world-wide community of 'fusioneers' building low-power fusors in their back bedrooms and garages with just a few readily available bits of equipment. Their work can be seen in videos on YouTube. Like me, I'm sure you'll be astonished.

To learn more, go to: fusor.net
Their comprehensive website is full of useful information for newbies and old hands alike.

In all likelihood, energy from stable fusion reactors built in huge laboratories at a cost of billions of dollars are inevitable.
On the other hand maybe somebody, somewhere, in a garage or basement, will stumble on a breakthrough – just like Harry Figg did.

What follows is a preview of Mark Wesley's novel, "BanGk!" The first in the James Stack, three book series.

JAMES STACK: Ex-Captain Special Forces, a tough, intelligent, risk taker, figured out that if you want to rob the Bank of England you don't go through the front door, guns blazing. You don't tunnel up through the floor either. You don't climb through windows, lower yourself on a harness, screw around with the computers, fix the security cameras, or play Twister with invisible Laser beams. You don't do any of that stuff because it won't work. That's why gold has never been stolen from the vaults of the Bank of England.

They've got every angle covered - except one.

A Few Golden Nuggets

4,600 tonnes of gold in the Bank of England (BoE)

Value: £187 billion / $315 billion

A 24 carat bar weighs 400 fine ounces (13.4kg) 28lbs

Each bar is worth approx. $520,000

80 bars per pallet

1 tonne per pallet

4 pallets to a rack

368 tonnes belong to the UK

Oldest gold bar in the vault was deposited in 1916

Foreign Custodial Gold Held in the Bank of England

Germany, Holland, Mexico, Austria, Australia, Ireland, Greece, Cyprus, India, Venezuela. Most of the old Commonwealth Countries. Many Middle East and Asian countries.

Prologue

London: The River Thames: Night

James Stack stood awkwardly on the narrow wooden hand-rail, balancing precariously against the rocking motion of the tourist boat. Only his one-handed grip on the rust encrusted steel-work of the deck above prevented him from falling overboard. The muzzle of a hand gun pushed hard into his back. The man with the gun wanted him to jump – 'Now!' Stack hesitated, but he knew he didn't have a choice.

Above him a brilliant display of fireworks was lighting up the night sky over Tower Bridge – its two majestic granite towers and ornate, cast-iron superstructure filling his horizon. Beneath it, scattered reflections of floodlight and fireworks danced on the surface of the dark waters of the Thames.

Unaware of the drama being played out on deck, a wild crowd in the saloon were partying noisily to the sound of a DJ playing an old Gloria Gaynor disco classic from the seventies.

Outside, Stack recognised the distinctive metallic *snick-click* of a round being chambered. Unmistakable, even over the noise from the disco. Then came another mean shove of the gun into his ribs and another menacing demand for him to jump.

A warm evening breeze had sprung up, carrying a wisp of acrid blue exhaust from the boats ancient diesel engines that caught in Stack's throat. He looked around. He couldn't see Charlie, so there was no way he could delay any longer.

He'd been in the risk business all his life, but if a bookie offered odds on who would survive, he'd put his money on Gloria.

This wasn't how the plan was supposed to go. Which left just one question – how the hell did he get himself into this mess?

Take the Money and Run

Eight months earlier

'Come on! For Christ's sake!' His voice was almost a whisper from the tension. He'd not been this stressed, even at the height of the fighting in Afghanistan. Your squad could be far from Camp Bastion, picking its way through the ruins of an abandoned village – dead of night – not sure if your next step would be your last. He'd been trained for it – that was the difference.

The driver's elbow rested on the sill of the open window, a half-smoked cigarette hung from his mouth, lit from the cigarette butt he'd flicked onto the road outside only few moments before. At least here, there were no snipers or IED's to contend with. It wasn't life or death. He took another anxious look at his watch.

The robbery was running late and the old Volvo had been parked up on the double yellows outside the bank far too long. Only people with disabilities who display the distinctive Blue Badge Permit on their vehicles are allowed to park on double yellow lines.

In this small town, mid-day, mid-week, and late summer, the high street resembled a ghost town. Only a handful made it in: mothers driving SUVs, pensioners using the rare bus service and those whose mobility was restricted but were still able to drive – the ones with the Blue Badge parking permits.

While he waited, one had arrived and parked in front. Shortly after, another had parked up behind him.

Only a moment ago, a female traffic warden had strolled over and signalled for him to move on. He pleaded with her that his heavily pregnant wife was in the bank and wouldn't be more than another minute.

In small market towns such as this, traffic wardens enlisted from the local population occasionally took a sympathetic view. She allowed him the extra time. He knew the good will was very time-limited. She could be on her way back now.

He checked in the mirror one more time. The beard worked if you didn't look too closely. The sun had finally come out and the day was warming up nicely, so the sun glasses didn't look out of place. What remained of the early morning shower, could be seen in the rapidly evaporating puddles lying here and there along the high street.

'*Come on guys!*' he hissed through clenched teeth, as he banged his gloved hands on the wheel in frustration.

At that moment, a dark shadow engulfed the Volvo as a vast fourteen-wheel bulk tipper truck drew noisily alongside, eclipsing the sun as it double parked next to him. Its driver, jumped down and ran across the road to a newsagent. The getaway car was now stuck between two parked cars and the DAF truck, the driver's door unable to open against a large, mud caked nearside wheel.

'What the hell...?'

He heaved himself across the seats and climbed out through the passenger door, ran out into the road and round to the driver's side of the truck. He checked the cab and up and down the main street, but the driver had vanished. His agitation increased when he looked at his watch and then to the bank. Still no sign of the other gang members.

He hesitated for a moment, unsure what to do, before climbing up into the cab. He checked up and down the high street again, but there was still no sign of the pain in the backside trucker. Sitting in the driver's seat he looked around the filth strewn cab and tentatively jiggled the gear stick while giving the other unfamiliar controls a cursory once over. The keys were still in the ignition and the engine was turning over noisily with the uneven clatter of an arthritic castanet player.

He looked up as two men rushed out of the bank. They ran straight to the getaway car but stopped dead when they noticed the huge red truck.

Hard to miss!

The driver leaned over and shouted down to them through the passenger window.

'Guys...change of bleeding plan!'

They rushed forward, clambered over the hood of their own car, pulled the cab door open, and squeezed into the passenger seat.

'Well, don't hang around. Let's go,' James Stack shouted with a profound sense of urgency, already adjusted to the new get-away plan.

The driver yanked and stirred the stick, before finally crunching it into first gear, causing the truck to kangaroo off, very nearly stalling. Eventually, with the old worn-out gear box whining and complaining, it picked up speed – lurching down the high street.

Across the road the truck driver was just leaving the newsagent with his newspaper, cigarettes, and a Snickers bar, when his pride and joy lumbered past. The screaming of gears mashing together sounding like wheel nuts being tightened by a compressed-air tool. He made a half-hearted attempt to run after it before coming to a standstill in the middle of the road waving his newspaper and hurling angry abuse – shocked at seeing his livelihood weaving dangerously from one side of the road to the other, eventually vanishing from sight over the brow of the hill at the far end of the old market-town. He stomped furiously back to the pavement, took out his phone and called the police.

On the edge of town, a compact Hyundai i10 police 'Panda' car was parked up outside a parade of shops. Inside, PC Evans was enjoying a late packed lunch of bacon and fried egg. Small drops of grease slid off his chin to join the other canteen medals staining his tunic as he stuffed his mouth full of his favourite savoury snack. That's when the radio crackled into life with an urgent all units shout from police HQ about the bank robbery and a stolen truck.

PC Evans threw his lunch onto the passenger seat, swallowed a mouthful of unchewed food in a painful gulp and grabbed the radio handset.

'Papa one–two. I'm in the neighborhood. Nothing suspicious to report.'

As the words left his lips, the truck barrelled noisily past: old plastic bags and newspaper pages billowing after it in the gust of its wake.

PC Evans was a careful man, not one of life's risk takers, which made the rigors of policing an odd career choice. Now, though, his face a study of fierce determination, he jammed the accelerator hard down to the floor. The Hyundai's tiny engine at first responded with insolent indifference, but then, grudgingly, picked up speed. He gave chase while providing a running commentary to Police Control.

'Proceeding down the high street. The truck's 100 yards ahead of me,' PC Evans said, all gung-ho and dogged resolve.

He wiped his sleeve across his greasy mouth and leaned forward into the chase.

Back in the truck, Toni 'Zero' Zeterio was giving the driver, Charlie 'Hollywood' Dawson, a hard time.

'Jesus Hollywood, couldn't you find something slower?' Zero shouted in panic above the noise of the engine. He rocked back and forth; eyes wide, mentally willing the truck to go faster. Hollywood took a quick drag on his cigarette before replying.

'What was I supposed to do, call the police and complain that some sod's double parked on the high street?'

'Leave him alone Toni,' Stack commanded. 'Just drive Charlie, there's a cop following us.'

'Yeah, it's only a little panda car. What's he going to do?' Hollywood said.

'Well right now he's telling the general police population of the UK where we are,' Stack explained patronisingly.

More crunching and lurching as Hollywood tried to find a higher gear.

Back in the panda, PC Evans attempted to keep up with the lorry, seen fleetingly ahead as it charged precariously down the narrow, winding country road.

'Just passing the cemetery, heading out of town towards Mrs Lumsden's boarding house and kennels.'

Police Control. 'I have no idea who or what that is.'

PC Evans. 'It's where we put Mavis when we go on holiday.'

'Mavis?'

'Our Cocker Spaniel.'

'Just tell us stuff we can recognise. *Click - buzz.* Then in a slow, patient voice. 'Listen, is there a sign for a town they're heading towards?'

'They might be heading towards the M1, so they could be heading towards London.'

'London is over fifty bloody miles away.' Exasperated, the voice of Police Control became sarcastically posh, 'Look, if you find a road sign that gives a clue as to where they might be going, do be sure to let us know, won't you?'

'Check. Will do,' PC Evans replied with renewed purpose as he reached for his discarded sandwich.

Back in the truck, Hollywood was pushing his driving skills to the limits.

'Yeah, the best car chase was in the French Connection. Did you see that? Bloody brilliant. Course, it wouldn't have worked with a truck would it? Mind you, Steve McQueen was great in Bullitt. You gotta love that Ford Mustang, I mean it's bloody marvellous ain't it. But all that 'Fast and

Furious' stuff, well it's all been done before hasn't it?'

His enthusiasm for the subject was endless – once he got started, Charlie 'Hollywood' Dawson could bore for Britain.

'For Christ sake, Hollywood,' Stack pleaded. 'Give it a rest and just drive.'

***

They'd set out with what seemed a novel, if perhaps simplistic, plan.

No guns. Definitely not. But the threat of violence couldn't be avoided to ensure compliance.

Stack had made an appointment to see the bank manager of a suitably remote regional bank, under the pretence of raising a business loan for a local commercial venture. For this scheme to work it was important that the manager's office was a separate private room, so some research had to be discretely undertaken.

Stack arrived at the appointed time. The manager introduced herself and invited him into her office, closed the door, and offered Stack a chair. She took her seat behind a small but stylish, glass and aluminium desk, upon which was laid out some printed material.

Stack went through the motions of raising a loan – at least to start with.

Outside, in the main bank area, Toni Zeterio was posing as just another customer waiting in line. Timing was important.

By the time he arrived at the window, the bank was empty apart from him and another customer further along the counter. The robbery began by holding a printed note flat against the glass partition for the clerk to see.

'DO NOT ACTIVATE THE ALARM. *Your manager is being held in her office. Use the phone, she will confirm this.* DO IT NOW.'

In the office, Stack steered the meeting away from the subject of temporary borrowing to a more permanent arrangement whereby the bank gives large quantities of cash to his accomplice outside. He told the manager to expect a phone call from one of the counter clerks and to provide the correct responses if she didn't want the clerk to come to harm. Stack's scheme relied on her choosing to play it safe rather than risk the health of her co-workers.

Meanwhile, in the front office, Toni waited for a reaction from the clerk.

Apart from a definite paling of skin colour as the blood drained from her face, she just sat there, frozen in place with her mouth open.

Toni gave her his most aggressive, threatening glare and an emphatic nudge of his head towards the phone on the shelves behind her.

That did the trick. She de-frosted, slid off her stool, went over to the phone, and did as the message directed. Her fingers trembling, she tapped out, 1...0...1, the manager's office number. Turning back to face Toni, she placed the handset to her ear and waited for her boss to answer.

It was just as the message said. The manager was being held under duress. She must not take any risks. Do exactly what they ask. She nodded her compliance to Toni and replaced the receiver.

He signalled for her to return to her place at the counter and pushed some cloth bags through the gap between the glass shield and counter. He then held a second instruction against the glass.

It was a simple and rather obvious next step: *'Fill the bags with cash, QUICKLY.'*

It was then that things started to fall apart. Noticing the unusual behaviour of his colleague, the other clerk left the customer he was serving and came over to find out what was going on. The woman stopped stuffing cash into the bag and looked up in panic, first at Toni and then at her colleague.

'Tell him,' Toni said in a threatening voice, disguised, he hoped, with a Liverpudlian accent.

He raised the first message to the glass again and gestured for the other clerk to read it, but the man just shook his head slowly and didn't move. Toni tried the threatening voice and reminded him of the danger his boss was in. Stubborn and defiant, the man merely folded his arms.

Toni didn't have time to screw around. He'd already got one bag full of cash, but the clerk, stuck in a loop of conflicting messages, had stopped filling the second bag.

'Don't just stand there, keep filling the bloody bag,' he growled at her with more than a hint of John Lennon.

She started doing just that, but 'superhero' came over, grabbed hold of the bag and began pulling on it. The woman clung on, desperately trying to stuff another handful of cash into it. The man gave it another hard tug and snatched it out of her hand, loose notes floating to the floor. Stalemate. Or more truthfully, checkmate!

Time to execute the next part of the plan: Exit the building and smartish.

'Time to go, Alpha,' he shouted in the direction of the manager's office.

Stack burst out of the office, following behind Toni who was already on his way through the automatic doors to the street.

They both ran towards the getaway car – and stopped dead. That's when they saw the truck.

***

While Charlie struggled to get more speed out of the old diesel engine, Toni Zeterio reached over and fiddled with another lever.

'What does this do, make it go faster? Is it another gear or something?' Toni asked.

'Don't know, let's give it a jiggle.'

Charlie glanced down momentarily, missing the road sign warning Low Bridge Ahead, as he yanked the lever back.

'Nothing seems to be happening.'

'Yeah, strange. Perhaps it's broken,' agreed Zero.

In the Panda, PC Evans noticed from a distance, that the shape of the truck seemed to be changing. It was getting taller!

Unseen by the three occupants in the cab as the truck careered along swinging wildly from side to side, the tipper body had started to rise, shredding branches from trees as it passed.

As they rounded a sharp left-hand bend, Hollywood saw the old brick railway bridge, half hidden by trees, its narrow arch already far too close.

Seconds later, as the large tipper body reached its highest point, the fourteen-wheeler rushed through the tunnel at high speed. The elevated bodywork smashed against the top of the bridge. The impact tore the tipper body away from its hydraulic mountings, leaving it teetering up-right on the road behind them.

Perhaps not surprisingly, with all the noise the old engine was making, and the shaking and rattling of the old chassis, the truck continued through the bridge and out the other side with only a small shudder marking the end of what for some years had been a productive relationship between the truck and its cavernous load bearing partner, an event noticed inside the cab as a sudden jolt that knocked Hollywood's cigarette butt out of his mouth. He did a cursory feel around his seat and on the cab floor between his legs for the burning remnant, but found nothing.

'What the hell was that?' Zero asked.

'Don't ask me mate,' Charlie said, adding, 'Could've been the drive shaft or something. Look at the mileage. It's already done over 245,000. It's knackered.'

'Well, something must have happened 'cause we've picked up a bit of speed for some reason.'

Stack looked through the side mirror.

'OK, I've got some good news and bad news. The bad news is we've lost the tipper bit at the back.'

'Where the hell did that go?' Charlie asked as he checked the door mirror.

And the good news?' asked Zero.

'That copper isn't following us anymore.'

Behind them, teetering precariously on its back end, the tipper body rocked tentatively for a moment before coming to rest, light as a feather, against the tunnel brickwork, the open space of its metallic void facing back down the road. A gaping mouth waiting for a victim. It didn't have long to wait.

Just seconds behind, hurtling round the sharp left-hand bend, PC Evans spotted the obstruction just in time to slam on the brakes.

The vast rectangular box of the tipper body quickly filled his windscreen. PC Evans gripped the steering wheel in terror and pushed down on the brake so hard his buttock clenching backside lifted off the seat. Somehow, he managed to slow the car enough that only the last faint dregs of forward momentum remained to push the front wheels slowly up, and come to rest on the raised lip of the tipper body. PC Evans just sat there in shocked silence – barely able to breathe – his hands still holding the wheel in a white knuckled death grip.

'Jesus!' he whispered somewhat prematurely. 'That was close!'

With the bulk of the engine sitting over the front axle, the weight of the car was just enough to cause the finely balanced tipper body to straighten up and begin an arc of travel that had just one inevitable conclusion.

It slowly started to keel over – several tonnes of tortured steel, moaning mournfully down towards the little Hyundai i10.

Horrified, PC Evans instinctively raised his hands to protect himself. He ducked down into his seat, looking up wide eyed into the darkening void that was falling down upon him.

Gravity finally won the argument as, with an enormous crash of metal on tarmac, the cavernous tipper body slammed down and engulfed the police car like a clam shell – clouds of dust, dirt, and leaves billowing up with the force of the impact.

Inside the Panda, all was dark and quiet except for static from the police radio. The dramatic change of circumstances left him stunned for a moment. His hand shook uncontrollably as he turned the headlight switch. Only one came on, its light reflected back through the fractured glass of the windscreen. He took a breath to bring his pounding heart rate under control, slowly reached for his radio handset, and clicked the transmit button.

'Hello control, this is Papa one-two, can you hear me? *Static*...Hello control, can you hear me? *Static*. I'm no longer following the truck. *Static*...Hello?...*Static*...Hello?...*Static*..'

***

The damaged vehicle had to be dumped as soon as possible.

They'd buried it deep in a thicket just off the road, after spotting a farm a short distance away. Half hidden amongst the trees, the house and out-buildings stood in their own small island of uncultivated meadow in the middle of rolling fields of late summer corn.

It didn't take them long to make their furtive way to the nearest barn and commandeer a rusting Ford Sierra. By some miracle the vintage heap burst into life after the second attempt. If it was insured, the owner could reclaim its value and buy himself a pizza.

ABOUT THE AUTHOR

After a lengthy broadcasting career, which included many happy years as a DJ on Radio Luxembourg, Mark Wesley enjoyed critical acclaim as a song writer and record producer.

Jingle composition and copy-writing for radio commercials followed, but his early love of film led him to launch the production company, Media Futures, which later evolved into, Mark Wesley Productions.

His first novel, BANGK! remains hugely popular, and was followed by FRACK! A tale of sabotage and greed.

Like the third instalment, 'DEAD CITY EXIT', they all feature his protagonist and allies; James

Stack, Charlie 'Hollywood' Dawson and the beautiful Canadian, Summer Peterson.

Mark is married with two children and two grandchildren. He lives in the rolling countryside of north west Essex.

Printed in Great Britain
by Amazon